DANCING IN THE SHADOWS

DANCING IN THE SHADOWS

Anne Saunders

CHIVERS
THORNDIKE

This Large Print book is published by BBC Audiobooks Ltd, Bath, England and by Thorndike Press®, Waterville, Maine, USA.

Published in 2005 in the U.K. by arrangement with the author

Published in 2005 in the U.S. by arrangement with Juliet Burton Literary Agency

U.K. Hardcover   ISBN 1–4056–3266–6 (Chivers Large Print)
U.K. Softcover   ISBN 1–4056–3267–4 (Camden Large Print)
U.S. Softcover   ISBN 0–7862–7425–5 (Nightingale)

The text of this Large Print edition is unabridged.
Other aspects of the book may vary from the original edition.

Set in 16 pt. New Times Roman.

Printed in Great Britain on acid-free paper.

British Library Cataloguing in Publication Data available

Library of Congress Cataloging-in-Publication Data

Saunders, Anne.
    Dancing in the shadows / by Anne Saunders.
      p.   cm.
    ISBN 0–7862–7425–5 (lg. print : sc : alk. paper)
    1. British—Spain—Fiction. 2. Women travelers—Fiction.
    3. Women dancers—Fiction. 4. Spain—Fiction. 5. Large type
books. I. Title.
PR6069.A88D36 2005
813'.54—dc22   2004029245

CHAPTER ONE

When her hired car broke down, Dorcas admitted to herself that it had been foolish of her not to stick to the beaten track. The hot Spanish sun dried her throat, and she was glad to find a patch of shade as she prepared for a lonely wait. This proved to be even longer than anticipated and despair was beginning to set in when a car came into sight.

It stopped in response to her frantic hand-wave, and a man climbed stiffly from behind the wheel. Rotund figure, bright flower-decorated shirt, his perspiring face wide in a smile. He—and his round-faced female companion—just had to be English!

How sweetly his straight-to-the-point: 'Help needed?' fell on her ears.

'That's the understatement of the year,' she admitted. 'I'm Dorcas West. My car has broken down. Do you know of a garage near here?'

'Passed one not too far back, my dear. *Garage Inglés.* They say it's run by an Englishman by the name of Tom Bennett. My name is Henry Brookes, and this is Martha, my wife.'

It was Martha Brookes who said: 'Let Henry have a look first. He knows quite a bit about cars.' As Henry obligingly delved beneath the

1

bonnet, her eyes whisked over Dorcas. Dorcas writhed under an expression that clearly deplored her lack of prudence in travelling alone.

The car defeated Henry. After a short consultation between husband and wife, Dorcas gratefully accepted the offer of a lift back to the garage. She hated troubling these nice people, especially as Henry Brookes kept glancing furtively at his watch, as if time was a vital factor.

She was relieved on their account, as well as her own, when Tom Bennett turned out to be a fair haired giant, with a wholesome manner that motherly Martha Brookes took to on sight.

Giving a small involuntary sigh, Martha Brookes said: 'I think we can safely leave you in Mr Bennett's dependable care. Goodbye, dear. Good luck.'

A salutary parting wish that was to look the other way. Dorcas was mercifully unaware of this as she turned to match Tom Bennett's friendly grin.

Tom took a note of the abandoned car's whereabouts, and nonchalantly left Dorcas in charge of his garage while he went to have a look at it. He returned with the car on the end of a tow rope.

'Not good?' she said, reading his expression.

'Rented job, you said?'

'Yes.'

'Some firms are quite reputable. Some wouldn't allow this heap of rubbish on the road.'

'As bad as that?' Dorcas questioned in dismay.

'Let's put it this way. Shall I phone the car hire firm and give them a few blistering comments, or will you?'

'You please, if you don't mind. I don't know any blistering comments. The language class I attended didn't teach us any.'

'It wouldn't. Want me to tell them to send a replacement car? Might be some delay. The recent rain, after that long dry spell, has caused a landslip and the main road is temporarily closed.'

'I wouldn't know about that. I haven't been sticking to the main road. Are the trains getting through?'

'At the moment, yes.'

'That would seem my safest bet. Don't bother about a replacement car. Just ask them to collect their property. I'll catch the train.'

'Wise girl,' he approved. He told her how to get to the station. Then added in friendly speculation: 'Not that I'm trying to hurry you away.'

'I really must go. How much do I owe you?'

'Forget it.'

'I paid the hire car fee in advance. There should be a refund. If there is, please keep it for your trouble,' she said punctiliously. He

3

reminded Dorcas of her brother, Michael. Which was odd because they weren't really alike.

Memory of her brother put a bar between her eyes, and Tom took this as a sign of rejection to his friendly overture. As his heart was already spoken for he thought that perhaps it was as well, and when Dorcas asked if there was anywhere she could get a cup of English tea, he directed her to Mama's Hacienda, assuring her that Mama made an excellent brew. He watched her walk bravely up the road, her suitcase bumping against her bare legs.

Tom had said Mama's Hacienda was the third villa past the monastery. She must have been mistaken because here it was and the monastery was beyond, on the rise of the hill. The foliage-laced, sparkling white villa was exactly as Tom had described it.

Voices drifted to her on a gentle breeze the moment before she spied the tables and chairs set in the chequered light and shade beneath a canopy of trees. She walked through the imposing wrought-iron gates, a presentiment of loneliness clutching at her throat, a feeling that her presence was an intrusion.

It will pass in a moment, she thought, brushing it off as her usual awkwardness when having to face strangers. And so many of them. It must be a very popular place. To her growing consternation, she saw there wasn't a vacant seat.

She stood, feeling lost and irresolute, not knowing whether to go or stay. Already she was collecting a fair share of attention. Her own glance chanced upon the regal-looking English lady presiding over a large silver teapot. Mama? Having a preconceived picture of a fat, homely señora firmly established in her mind, she felt slightly cross with Tom Bennett for not warning her that Mama was a compatriot.

This very unlikely-looking Mama enquired in highly cultured English: 'Yes? Did you want something?'

'Tea, please,' said Dorcas meekly and was unprepared for, and a little hurt by, the ripple of laughter her request brought. Hating to be so very much in the limelight, she darted the gallant Spaniard who offered her his seat a look of undying gratitude. She dare not look at him properly, not yet, until her embarrassment had evaporated a little.

'Tea for the señorita,' she heard him say. And shortly afterwards a welcome cup of tea was handed to her.

Her Spanish gallant procured an extra chair from somewhere and asked permission to join her. Dorcas nodded. In the circumstances she could hardly do otherwise.

He spoke excellent English and as she raised her eyes for the first time, she began to doubt her original hurried assessment of his

5

nationality. He was tall, even by English standards, and his skin wasn't as dark as a Spaniard's, although he had a Spaniard's arrogant features. It was a bold, challenging face; a face with the medieval quality one finds in the well-preserved portraits that hang in art galleries. But the well-defined mouth was that of a modern-day buccaneer. And the eyes, unexpectedly the blue of a midnight sky, contained a most indecorous twinkle.

She sipped her tea, feeling more disconcerted by his gaze than the collective gazes of everybody else around her. She wondered, inconsequently, where he'd got his dark blue eyes from.

'I did not expect to see so many people,' she said conversationally.

'These are my parents' friends. They are here to celebrate my parents' thirtieth wedding anniversary.'

Dorcas's cheeks flushed a brighter red than the blood-red roses on the table.

'Wedding anniversary!'

She should have suspected something like this. For one thing, everybody was dressed for an occasion. No way did they resemble the usual oddly garbed collection of tourists. And, of course, this explained the stares and amused glances.

She drew in an agonized breath. 'I'd no idea I'd gatecrashed a private party. I didn't know Mama's Hacienda wasn't open for normal trade.'

Worse was to follow.

'Mama's Hacienda?' His surprise turned to amusement. 'I see!'

And quite suddenly Dorcas saw too.

'This isn't Mama's Hacienda?'

'No. This is the residence of the Señores Ruiz. The distinguished looking bearded gentleman is Enrique Ruiz, my papa. My mother is Rose Ruiz. She is English, as you are probably aware. I am Carlos Ruiz, although I answer just as happily to Charles, the English equivalent of my name.'

Dorcas realized he wanted some return for all that information. She reasoned this out very slowly because her mind was still in shock. 'Oh . . . yes . . . please forgive me. I'm still reeling. What a dreadful mistake to make. I'm Dorcas West. And I must go.'

'I offend you by laughing.' He sobered instantly. 'I am not laughing at you.'

'That's very nice to hear, but I'm still . . .'

'I am smiling at the benevolence of the kindly fate that directed your steps. Please stay.'

In her struggle for composure, she was clumsily honest. 'This isn't fate-planned. This is the hand of human error. Mine.'

'Don't you believe in fate?' he said with dry audacity. The impression being that he was challenging her to believe in something he regarded with scepticism.

7

'No, I don't.' Yet . . . absurdly . . . it was as if an unknown force had brought her here, and that a step taken today could never be retraced.

The dark blue sorcerer's eyes teased her gullibility. It hardly seemed fair, not when these same eyes were guiding her into this area of thought. It was weak of her to allow her mind to be manipulated in this way. She should break free and run; yet she sat motionless, hardly daring to breathe for fear of breaking this—yes!—enchanted spell her common-sense was frantically denying.

She must have moved, must have obeyed the feeble spark of rebellion and made some effort to escape, because his hands were easing her back into her chair.

'You can't go until you have told me all about yourself. There is something about you I find intriguing.'

Her hands fidgeted on her lap.

'You are . . .' His brow creased as his mind plundered his brain for the word . . . 'an enigma. A sealed book whose pages would make a fascinating perusal. I do not embarrass you?'

'No,' she lied, choking on his effrontery. Who wouldn't be embarrassed!

'You are so English,' he said. 'As English as the rose, and tea in delicate china cups.'

'Yes.'

'I am half English,' he said, with a

8

Spaniard's pomposity that widened her smile into a laugh.

Her gaze escaped past his to the *ama de casa*, Rose Luiz, this disturbing man's English mother. 'You've got your mother's eyes.'

'And whose eyes have you got, Dorcas?' He used her name naturally, without familiarity. 'Sherry-gold eyes.' He reached up as if to touch them, but his fingertips drew circles round them in the air. 'And the smallness and grace of a gazelle. You are well-named. Who have you to thank for such foresight?'

'My father chose my name. In Greek, Dorcas means gazelle, as you obviously know.'

She turned her chin from the penetration of his gaze. His hand lightly touched her cheek, flooding it with colour. 'I wonder if you know how beautiful you are.'

She made herself remember that all Spaniards flattered to the point of exaggeration. Very probably he was saying what he thought was expected of him. It did not cross her mind that he could be flirting with her—showing unwarranted interest in her personal background—out of kindness. Certainly, if his intention was to take her mind off her *faux pas*, he was one hundred per cent successful. Her embarrassment in his interest made her forget she was an interloper.

'I am not beautiful,' she declaimed. 'My brother is beautiful. I am insignificant beside him.'

9

'Is your brother travelling with you?'

'No. He is touring France. I chose to holiday in Spain. I am alone.' Should she have said that? Was it wise to advertise her vulnerability?

'What are your parents thinking of?'

'My parents are dead.' Her voice was so low it barely stirred the silence.

Quick concern touched his features. 'I'm sorry. I've brought the shadows to your eyes. The last thing I intended was to bring back a sad memory.'

'It happened a long time ago. Ten years to be exact.' Her voice was softly forgiving. 'They were killed in a plane crash.'

'Ten years ago you must have been little more than a baby. Who brought you up?'

'Grandmother. She never let us feel deprived. My brother Michael and I were lucky to have such a kindly, understanding parent substitute.'

Even though a winter and a spring had passed, it was still too recent not to invoke bitter and painful memories. She remembered everything of that night, from the moment her key grated in the lock. Beyond the threshold, her brother Michael had been waiting to impart the news.

'Grandmother has been taken ill. A stroke, apparently. The doctor is with her now. At this stage it's difficult to tell how severe, but it looks pretty bad.'

10

Then Doctor Chandler was coming towards her. 'Go to her, quickly, child.'

'Of course, Doctor. Coming Michael?'

'No.' Her brother's face contorted, and she saw the heightened colour in his cheeks which linked with the glass of whisky in his hand. 'I've gone to her for the last time. All her life she's had the whip hand. I'll be damned if I'll go running to her in death.'

'What a thing to say! How can you be so cruel and unfeeling? Michael!' she implored. But her brother turned from her, and Dorcas went to the sick-room alone.

It was a long and lonely vigil. She couldn't face food. What little sleep she had was taken curled up in the high-backed, blue velvet chair, within sight of the ivory and gold counterpane.

Michael looked in occasionally, his head buzzing as he speculated the size of his inheritance. He knew exactly what he intended to do with the money. Dorcas was shocked beyond belief.

'Grandmother is still alive. How can you plan what to do with her money! How can you talk as if she's already dead!' His callousness and greed appalled her more than anything she had experienced in her life.

Just before the end, as sometimes happens, her grandmother rallied, briefly easing the presentiment of death. For a short while she seemed almost her old lucid self. 'Where is Michael?' she asked.

11

'He's been here all the time you were asleep,' Dorcas lied lovingly. 'He just slipped out for a moment.' Perhaps she didn't lie too well at that, because the old eyes were darkly condemning. 'Don't be too harsh.' The skeletal fingers closed round Dorcas's wrist. 'Just because he's prettier than you are, don't spite the boy. I've no time for petty jealousy. Never have had.' Then she said querulously: 'Where is Michael? Where is my beautiful boy? We've all spoilt him, you know. It's not his fault if we've spoilt him, is it?'

'No, Grandmother, it isn't,' Dorcas had said, struggling not to be hurt by the unjust criticism.

With perfect timing Michael returned, his face a pale slash of concern at the doorway. Dorcas had risen stiffly and stood to one side, her twisting fingers hidden behind her back. She'd always stood aside for Michael. Grandmother was wrong. She adored her golden brother along with everyone else. She wasn't jealous of him.

Michael's hand tapped her shoulder. 'It's all over. The old girl's gone.' His matter-of-fact tone nauseated her. As the violent tears slid down her cheeks, pinging like needles on her clenched fists, she knew that somehow she must make a life for herself without her brother.

She didn't anticipate difficulty, and she met none. When she told him her decision to 'go it

12

alone' he seemed quite relieved.

Grandmother hadn't left any money, just the tall, dignified house, which she had willed to Michael. Predictably, he decided to sell. Dorcas got rid of what possessions wouldn't fit into a suitcase and this she dragged with her, resting it briefly in a series of drab lodging houses as she tried to carve a career for herself in the one thing she did with any degree of fluidity and grace. She was a dancer. On the stage her awkwardness vanished and her fey personality and swift gazelle purity of movement captured the attention of the audience. But she was the first to admit that she lacked that special something that is hard to define, the plus element that assures stardom. In both her home and her working life she followed the same inescapable pattern. It seemed she was destined to dance for ever in the shadow of someone else's brilliance.

A finger and thumb snapped under her nose. 'Please come back,' said Carlos. 'I do not like conversing with a stone.'

'I'm sorry. You were saying?'

'No. You were saying. You were telling me about yourself. I am desolate to realize you are so alone. What is your brother thinking of shirking his responsibilities! He should not allow you to wander like a waif.'

'Can one be a waif at twenty-two?'

'Are you? I had wondered. And set you a year or so under. I am pleased you are twenty-two. A woman.'

'Who should still be under the protection of her brother?' she said, a puckish smile teasing up her mouth.

'You mock. But yes, that is what I think. A son of Spain would honour such a responsibility.'

'That has a tyrannical ring to it that sets my teeth on edge. I should object most forcibly to being protected. Protection is so often another word for domination. I should hate to be dominated and told where I may go and what I am permitted to do, which I think is what you mean by honouring a responsibility. I am glad you are not my brother.'

'I second that most heartily.' His tone was dry. 'In view of my thoughts, that would be a most improper thing to be.'

With commendable dignity, Dorcas said: 'It is time I went.'

'And risk engendering fate's disapproval?' he teased inventively. 'Fate is a woman who does not like to be crossed. Think of all the trouble she must have taken to arrange this meeting between us.'

His chin was tilted in arrogance, his blue eyes were brilliant in laughter. Dorcas found him dangerously attractive. A greater proportion of English reserve, a smaller helping of Spanish charm, would have produced a more manageable man. But not such an interesting one, was the renegade

14

thought.

Sighing, she rose to her feet. 'Thank you for the tea. Goodbye.'

'If you are determined to go, I cannot stop you.' His smile was philosophical. 'The world is not such a big place and it is shrinking daily. Perhaps . . .' The implication that they would meet again was as empty as the air it trailed into.

He could not mean the regret his tone conveyed. Flattery was a basic Spanish trait. Relish it, then relinquish it. Prudently observing this thought, Dorcas dragged back the hand given to him in goodbye and bent to pick up her suitcase.

'Let me take that. Allow me to drive you somewhere.'

'No. Thank you but that won't be necessary.' The only voice at her command had husky undertones. 'I'm perfectly capable of carrying my own suitcase.' She straightened her shoulders, as if to strengthen her independence.

His smile no longer seemed quite so arrogant. 'As you wish.' His rueful expression dimmed his Don Juan image. He looked— yes—unhappy to see her go.

Dorcas walked away imprinting it all in her mind. The blending of scents drifting on the breeze, the wild non-uniformity of colour spilling joyously from the flower urns skirting the steps. Colours fade, scents evaporate;

15

Dorcas knew that Carlos Ruiz would stay brilliant in her mind for some time to come.

The sun ploughed into a bank of cloud, plunging the hazy gold overtones of the day into premature twilight. She had the strange, soul-sinking sensation of walking away from light and laughter.

* * *

On arrival at the railway station, Dorcas looked round for a seat in expectation of a long wait. Spanish trains were slow and often late. Neither were they all that frequent.

She was fretful and on edge. Leaving her suitcase, she walked the length of the platform, then resumed her seat. Her normal command of patience was conspicuously absent.

One moment she was quite alone on the platform, the next it was swarming with people. She identified them as a break-away dozen or more of the Ruiz party.

She pressed her shoulders against the hard platform seat, as though wishing to disappear into it. Silly of her, because had Carlos Ruiz intended to follow her, he would have done so straight away. Also, he would have come alone.

No great mystery. The reason they were here turned out to be the obvious one. To wish godspeed to a girl of about her own age, a girl blessed with luxuriant black hair and sparkling

16

eyes. She had a champagne personality, bubbling over with animation. Words effervesced from her lips.

'I've had such a *wonderful* time. I have so much to tell my dear Jaime when I get home. Yes, I wish I could have stayed longer. No . . . no . . . I will not be persuaded to change my mind. I have already been parted too long from my dearest husband. My heart aches at the absence . . . besides which, my Jaime is too attractive and has the too plausible tongue to be left on his own.'

This sage-tinged witticism received its expected laugh, and then Rose Ruiz came into the limelight with an imploring: 'But Feli, my child, I beg you to reconsider. In a few days the road will be open and your brother will be only too pleased to drive you home. The train journey is so tedious. Think how much more pleasant it will be by car.'

Was the 'my child' a figure of speech, or was Feli her daughter? Was Carlos the brother Señora Ruiz referred to? More to the point, was Carlos here?

Dorcas searched faces until her eyes felt screwed-out and sore; then the sound of that memorable voice directed her head.

'Mother is right. It would be more sensible to stay until I can drive you home.' But his words were flat and without command, and he gave his sister but scant attention. It was as if he were aware of Dorcas's scrutiny and his

17

head was alerted for sight or sound of her.

Dorcas was on the point of coming out of the shadows and revealing her presence when two white arms slid up and fastened round his neck. A voice, husky with meaning, demanded: 'Can love ever be sensible, Carlos? Is it not natural for Feli to want to hasten to her man? As any woman does, for that matter. Are you so cold that your heart does not beat faster at the thought?'

He replied: 'Isabel, you may hasten to me any time you wish.'

Strain as she might, Dorcas could only get a tantalizing back view of the daring Isabel. And Carlos's two hands clasped proprietorially round her incredibly slender waist.

So! It was exactly as she had surmised. His English blood had not diluted his aptitude for meaningless Spanish flattery. What had passed between them had no greater significance than an English wink or a wolf whistle. While she was in Spain, Dorcas would do well to remember that unlike his English counterpart, the Spanish male makes a gala performance of a simple act of appreciation.

The train drew in. Dorcas slipped unobtrusively aboard. Feli scrambled on breathless seconds before it started to move. From the door she blew kisses and goodbyes, and began to progress totteringly along the swaying carriage. Her eyes were still turned in on happy thoughts so that although she chose

18

to sit opposite Dorcas, she did not actually see her. The baby, a girl, gurgled in her arms and pushed her fat feet against Feli's flat stomach.

Dorcas gasped in spontaneous delight. 'I didn't know about the baby! I didn't see her.'

'Why should you know about my baby?' Feli enquired, puzzled. 'I do not think we are acquainted.'

Afraid lest Feli thought she was too pushing, Dorcas drew back. 'No. I witnessed the leave-taking just now.'

'Papa was holding Rosita. She is the light of his life. The second best flower in his garden.'

'Rosita? What a pretty name.'

'Mama, the flower of his existence, is Rose. My little one just had to be Rosita. Little Rose.'

'How charming. And so is she. You must be very proud of her.'

'Beware. That is a most imprudent remark. I am tempted to answer at great length. I am told I can talk for hours on the subject of my daughter. Or any other subject for that matter. In the family circle I am called a chatter-box. Are you certain we are not acquainted? I feel that we've met somewhere . . . quite recently.'

'I hardly think that likely,' Dorcas put in quickly. 'I should have felt it too.'

'Yes. Of course you are right. Are you visiting friends? Or are you on holiday?'

'I'm on holiday. I decided rather late and the package tours of my choice were fully

19

booked, so I'm doing it the adventurous way.'

'And is it? Adventurous?'

'It has not been without trauma. I hired a car and it broke down on me. I decided to continue my sightseeing by train.'

'A most wise decision,' said Feli, nodding over the baby's head, 'considering the havoc wrought by the recent rain. Have you been to Spain before?'

'No. This is my first visit.'

'*Caramba!*' exclaimed Feli, waving her free hand in a gesture of dismay. 'You came for the sun and found the tempest. What a dreadful first visit. I've never known such torrential rainfall. I don't wonder that landslips have made the roads impassable. That was a violent storm we had last night. Did you manage to get any sleep?'

'No. As I lay in bed I felt that at any moment a thunderbolt was about to crash through the roof of the hotel. Finally I got up and sat it out by the window. I've never seen lightning at such close quarters before. I could quite clearly make out the forked shape. It was scary, unreal. I've never seen anything so spectacular or as frightening in my life. I could hardly believe it when the sun blazed in the sky this morning. I think that's what unnerved me.' And made her susceptible to later events.

'The contrast, you mean? We are a country of sharp contrasts. Light and shade. Cruelty and kindness. We love and we quarrel in

20

practically the same breath.' Triumphant recognition darted across her features. 'I am right! I knew I was. We have met before, and I've remembered where!'

Feli's smile deepened; so did the colour in Dorcas's cheeks.

'I see I must own up. I gate-crashed your parents' anniversary party.'

'You were not unwelcome. On the contrary, you were most welcome to stay. Why did you run away? What did my wicked brother say to make you go in such a hurry?'

'Nothing. I found your brother quite charming.'

The stiffness in her voice drew a perceptive: 'Ah! Too charming, perhaps?'

'That seems to infer he is too charming to a lot of females. But perhaps he is more charming to one than the others?' Her probing was rewarded.

'You mean Isabel? He won't marry her. Papa won't press it for one thing, because he is too much of a romantic. It would please Mama. It would unite two old families and two family businesses. Isabel's family are also wine merchants. Carlos won't marry her for that. He has not officially asked for Isabel. He's always teased her and told her that he's waiting for her to grow up, but that's not the same, is it?'

'Don't you want Isabel for a sister-in-law?'

'No. How blunt that sounds. Don't

21

misunderstand me, she is a dear girl, no one could wish for a sweeter friend, but I feel it in my heart that she is not right for Carlos.' Impulsively, Feli reached forward and touched Dorcas's hand. 'Now that we've met, do not slip away. Will you spend part of your holiday with me? We have too many empty rooms, and my Jaime will be delighted to meet you. He likes me to have company.'

Dorcas felt the silken thread of fate very gently pulling her in. It would have been so easy to say yes. She genuinely liked Feli, and if she were honest with herself she didn't want to lose touch with Carlos's family. But there was something too planned about the whole thing. Something that caught like a scream in the throat. Something as frightening and forbidding as the thing we don't understand, like the storm she had lived through last night. It had drawn her and terrified her, so that while every nerve craved to huddle under the illusory safety of the bedclothes, she had squared her chin and gone out to meet it. She was not a coward.

She shook her head to clear it. This wasn't the same thing at all. And so, for the second time, she denied fate.

'I'm sorry,' she informed Feli, smiling regretfully, 'but I must say no to your kind offer. There is so much of Spain that I've promised myself to see that there won't be any time to squeeze in a visit to you.'

'It was just an idea,' Feli said wistfully. 'You must follow the dictates of your heart.'

Dorcas thought that if she did that she would be accepting the invitation, not declining it.

The sky darkened with terrifying swiftness. It was as if some enraged power, showing its displeasure, had contemptuously flung a cloak over the earth.

Feli shivered. 'We're going to have another storm. I hate storms.'

The baby absorbed her mood and began to whimper.

'Now, now,' said Dorcas in brisk, jollying-round tones. 'We mustn't look on the—'

'Dark side?' said Feli, casting her frightened eyes up at a sky that was getting blacker by the second. 'There have been reports of tornadoes seen off the southern coastline. Weird tunnels of wind sucking up everything in sight.'

'Now stop that,' Dorcas admonished sharply. 'This is just a storm. Most likely it will die out as quickly as it started.'

The sky was now so black it was the colour of pitch. The rain started to fall like some terrible vengeance, ceaselessly beating and flattening the vineyards and olive groves, tormenting the deepening spread of trees and a lone farmstead that valiantly clung to the side of a hill.

The rails sliced down into a valley where there were more vineyards, and the wind rivalled the rain until there was little to see of the whipped, tossed, wet countryside. Thunder rolled down the mountains. A blue light, like the blue-white flash of a camera flashgun, illuminated the carriage, picking out Feli's stone-tense features and those of the whimpering child.

Aggressively cheerful, Dorcas reached into her handbag.

'Have a mint.' Anything to snap Feli out of her frozen inertia. 'Not you, sweetie.' Pressing a finger against Rosita's button nose. 'Can the little one have some chocolate?'

'What?' Feli's eyes were as blank as her voice.

'Chocolate. Can Rosita have some? Inclined to be messy.'

'Yes of course. I'm not one of those fussy parents,' said Feli, momentarily snapping out of it, and accepting the broken-off piece of chocolate. 'I'm being silly, aren't I?'

Dorcas, not feeling too brave herself, was keenly sympathetic. 'We all have our hang-ups. Look, the sky is brightening. The storm is abating, just as I said it would.' She heaved a sigh of relief. She was beginning to feel like a spent force herself.

Too much had happened in too short a time. She was as much mentally as physically cramped to the point of exhaustion. Too many things had played on her emotions. Her grandmother's death had been a cruel blow.

Her grandmother had filled a large part of her life and she still couldn't believe that she would never see her again. Apart from losing a loved one, Dorcas had been faced with the upheaval of leaving home for the uncertainty of finding temporary accommodation and never properly unpacking her suitcase. The strain of rehearsals and the fight to keep on her dancing toes in a competitive field. All this on top of the heartache of discovering that her brother Michael had a hard, greedy side to his nature that was difficult to forgive.

Grandmother had spent as she lived, leaving only the house and its contents. At first Dorcas had been hurt that she hadn't been remembered in the will, until she reasoned it out in her mind that her grandmother had assumed that Michael would keep on the house and provide Dorcas with a home there. But Michael had sold the house and contents. Dorcas didn't want a share of the proceeds. She had her pride. But it would have comforted her to be offered something. She was not too proud to ask for a memento of her grandmother. 'Of course,' Michael said obligingly when asked. 'I didn't think. Take anything you want.' 'If I may, I'll have this,' and she picked up her grandmother's well-thumbed bible.

The sky was darkening again. For a moment Dorcas thought the storm was returning. Then she realized the train was travelling in the

25

shadow of a range of mountains. She disliked the mountains. They blocked out the remaining bit of daylight and she felt menaced. Rosita was still fretful. Dorcas offered to hold her for a while. Feli gladly handed over her precious burden. The child gazed up at Dorcas disbelievingly; her eyes were like twin moons. There was a chocolate smear down the side of her mouth. She stared at Dorcas for a long moment, wondering whether to accept her or not. Finally she gave an aggrieved snuffle and settled her head against Dorcas's breast. Dorcas could feel her breathing; the warmth of conquest mingled with the wonder of the child's perfection. She was sorry to hand Rosita back to her mother.

There was a distant rumbling sound, and the feeling of menace gripped Dorcas once again, only it was fiercer now. Feli's and Rosita's cheeks were glued together; Feli was smooth-talking her daughter to sleep. The rumbling sounded again, nearer, like thunder, and not like thunder. Dorcas found herself struggling to identify the sound, recognizing its importance with the sense of self-preservation.

She was sitting up, tense, alert, waiting. The train seemed to be reducing speed, as if it too was hesitant to plough into danger. Or were her taut nerves playing tricks? No, the train was slowing, she was quite certain of that. And the rumble of thunder, that was not thunder, filled her ears.

26

She knew she had to move. Quickly. She was acting on instinct alone. She couldn't give Feli a plausible explanation. Feli could not heed the danger and was reluctant to move. 'Stretch your legs if you want to. I'm perfectly all right here.'

'It's not that. I think we should all go to the end of the train. There's a fair chance that we might be safe there.'

'Safe? What are you talking about? Safe from what?'

Dorcas couldn't tell her because she didn't know herself. She only knew she had to get Feli and Rosita to the end compartment. The urgency of the presentiment that was driving her, robbed her of simple speech. She must not panic. She must stay cool. Her eyes were eloquent of all the things she could not find words for. Success at last! She could tell by the changing expression on Feli's face that she had managed to transmit her fears. For the first time she blessed her 'talking' eyes.

'I'll come with you. I don't know why, but if it matters to you that much, I'll come.' So saying, Feli got to her feet.

They began to walk. They were only two thirds down the train when it happened. Rocks started to smash against the carriage windows. The floor quivered alarmingly beneath them. The mountainside was crumbling. It was coming down on them in an avalanche of rock and sludge.

27

Feli screamed. *'Madre mia!* It's a landslide.'
Rosita was clutched tightly in Feli's arms.
Dorcas's arms went round both of them. The
instinct now was to protect. The train
screeched to a stop. The thunder of the
collapsing mountainside went on . . . and on . . .
and on. A dull, reverberating boom . . . boom
. . . boom . . .

CHAPTER TWO

They had been thrown to the floor of the carriage, which seemed to be tilted at an angle. In assessing the situation, Dorcas thought she might have come off worse. Her leg was trapped. She must have acted as a sort of buffer for Feli and Rosita. Feli's mouth quivered between laughter and tears. Dorcas didn't need medical knowledge to know she was in a state of shock.

Rosita's face crumpled and she let out a great sobbing wail as blood appeared from nowhere and began to trickle down her forehead. Dorcas ignored the stinging pain in her leg and by reaching out as far as she could, managed to collect up the hurt little girl. Rosita was too tiny to be caught up in such a frightening situation. It seemed very important to wipe the blood away before Feli saw it. Dorcas rummaged for her handkerchief and wiped away the sticky wetness before it got into Rosita's eyes. She dabbed at the poor mite's forehead until it became apparent it was only a superficial scratch.

Rosita looked up at Dorcas, regarding her for an endless moment with her huge moon eyes. Her expression was very still and serious as she considered the situation. When you are that young it's terrifying to have the world tip you upside down and then find yourself in a stranger's arms. She gave Dorcas a look as if to say, 'Oh, it's you again', and snuggled close. Dorcas felt justifiably smug and would have been content to continue rocking Rosita to and fro as she whispered indiscriminate soothing noises in her ear. Only:

'Feli. Would you mind taking charge of your daughter. I think I'm going to faint.'

*   *   *

What happened next wasn't very clear to Dorcas. In fact she remembered little of the next seven days. Someone told her it was seven days, otherwise she wouldn't have known. To her it was a long, drugged hiatus. The only time things were clear was when she felt the pain. They gave her something and the pain went, and so did clarity.

She knew she had hurt her leg. She knew she was in hospital. She thought Feli and Rosita were all right because every time she asked, a chin—not always the same chin—bobbed up and down. And there was a hand by the bed, and that was always the same hand. It stayed there day and night, ever constant, giving her all the assurance she needed. She had only to put her hand out to have her fingers gripped and held. It was a big hand. Her own disappeared into it with room to spare. She felt small and fragile and the hand

30

was big and comforting. It protected and enclosed her in its strength. She never stopped to ask herself who the hand belonged to. That wasn't important. The fact that it was there when she needed it was enough.

And sometimes, when the world was wrapped in a night stillness, a pair of lips would brush her cheek, and her throat would close on tenderness. She was aware of talking a great deal. An urgency of words bubbled from her. She had no idea what she was saying and was too dazed to worry about whether she was being indiscreet. She gabbled on and on, encouraged by soft, male murmurs. And the hand did warm, intimate things to hers. It stroked the inside of her wrist and played with her fingers.

Then she was better, sitting up and appreciating her visitors. Feli and Rosita were among the first. Feli stared at her with shiny, grateful eyes while Rosita scrambled all over her bed, and ate her chocolates and grapes.

'I'm pleased to see the patient looking so much better,' said Feli.

'You mean you've been before?'

Feli rolled her eyes. 'Everybody's been before. Carlos. Mama and Papa.' And then a small, tearing sob came from her throat. 'How can I ever thank you, Dorcas. You saved our lives.' She scooped up Rosita and pressed her close, as though to blot out the horror. 'If you hadn't insisted we move, we would have been

31

in the part of the railway carriage that was completely wrecked. And if you hadn't bothered with us, you could have got clear yourself and you wouldn't be lying in hospital now.'

Dorcas pleated the bedspread. She hated praise and didn't know how to deal with it. She protested that she had done no more than anybody would have done in the circumstances. But Feli wouldn't have it.

'That's not true, Dorcas. You didn't have one thought of self. Your only concern was for us. I feel so bad that you are having to pay so terribly for your kind deed.'

Feli's papa, Enrique Ruiz, came to see her next.

He said: 'Well, Dorcas,' and smiled at her.

He was not very tall. His chin sported a neatly trimmed, slightly imperious looking black beard, and his liquid black eyes contained a wily gleam. Easy to imagine him resorting to cunning and trickery and every stratagem in the book to get his own way. But at the same time there was something endearing about him so that one wouldn't mind being inveigled by such a charming rogue. No wonder Carlos's English mother had been won over.

Dorcas felt at ease with him—another facet of his charm—and her shoulders relaxed perceptibly. There were so many questions she had to ask that it would be helpful to have a sympathetic ear. But first she looked at his hands. They were a gentleman's hands with neatly clipped and manicured nails. His fingers were slim and he wore a wedding ring, in accordance with the Spanish custom, on his right hand. A hand that wasn't much larger than her own.

'Señor, while I was ill, someone stayed with me. Was it a member of the hospital staff?'

'You have been attentively looked after by the staff, but you may be referring to my son. Carlos was anxious about you, as we *all* were.' Did he stress this point? 'He chose to chart your progress himself.'

So it had been Carlos. She lay back on her pillow. She almost wished Señor Ruiz would go so that she could capture again the sweetness of those moments. And yet, she was half afraid they had never happened. Oh, Carlos had sat with her all right. But could she be sure his fingers had traced her wrist and lovingly caressed each finger in turn? How could she know that aspect of the situation had not been drug induced?

Enrique Ruiz was saying: 'I am right, I think, in sensing that you are not the person to want speeches and bouquets. However, I cannot let the moment pass without mentioning the depth of our gratitude. Feli is our only daughter, little Rosita is precious beyond words. Thank you, Dorcas.' His eyes were now liquid with tears. 'We rejoice that you are now well. Laughter was scarce in our household while you were so ill. What more can I say? What can I give you? Is there anything you desire?'

'I want to go home.'

'Home? You mean England?'

'Yes, señor.'

'In a big aeroplane?' The eyes narrowed in tease, then in kindness. 'It is not possible, even if we were content to let you go. You are not well enough to tackle the flight, even supposing you had someone to look after you at the other end.' Answering the pained look in Dorcas's eye, he explained: 'I made it my business to look into your background.'

'What did you find, señor?'

'Your only relative is a brother who is at the moment somewhere in France. We are trying to locate him through the French police. He has a right to know what is happening to his sister.'

As if he would care, thought Dorcas, her mouth sliding into hurt.

'Meanwhile, arrangements have been made for you to convalesce at my home, the Villa Serena. I hope you will find—' A pause; a smile '—serenity and happiness there. Certainly, I and my family will do everything possible to make your stay enjoyable.'

'You are too kind, señor,' said Dorcas, dismayed at her own meek acceptance. But what else could she do? She couldn't walk away. Not on these legs.

Following her glance, Enrique Ruiz became briskly practical. 'It can be arranged for a local nurse to come to the villa to dress your leg. How is the leg, by the way?'

'Stiff, señor. I've been told it will be at least twelve months before it can regain its normal strength.'

She tried to say this as naturally as possible. She couldn't be sure how deeply Señor Ruiz had probed into her background. If he knew she was a dancer, he would know damage to her leg was the worst possible blow that could befall her. If she was out of circulation for a year, she could consider her dancing career at an end. She would have to look to some other means of employment to earn her living. She didn't want the señor and his family to know this. She didn't want them to feel more beholden to her than they already did.

'There is something bothering you that we haven't touched on yet. Please tell me what it is,' Enrique Ruiz demanded in crisp but kind enquiry.

'You are very perceptive, señor. I won't deny there is something. I've asked the doctors and nurses several times, but they sweep my enquiry aside as something of no consequence, which it is. I do not like to tell you in case you think me vain.'

'A woman entirely without vanity is like a flower without a scent. For me, a flower

35

without a scent has no appeal whatsoever. Tell me what is troubling you.'

'I know it is trivial and small-minded of me, but . . . will I carry a scar on my leg? At the moment the skin is puckered and it is very ugly. Will it always be like this?'

'Ah!' His mouth pursed. 'If you were a man, it would not matter. But a pretty young woman cannot be content to hide her legs beneath long skirts for ever. It is true that you will carry the scar for a while. Time will fade it.' His voice sounded far from convincing, and a tuck appeared between his eyebrows. 'And if it doesn't, no matter. Have you never heard of cosmetic surgery?'

'I have heard of it, señor. I have heard it comes expensive.'

'That is the least of your worries. You might have been foolhardy in flawing your skin to save my kin, but at least you had the good sense to put a wealthy family in your debt. That was meant as a joke,' he said, as a stricken look came to Dorcas's eyes.

Dorcas had no wish to take from these good people. Already she had tasted generously of the Ruiz wealth. Her own suitcase had not been located in the wreckage and she was coming to terms with the fact that it might never be reclaimed. The nightgown she was wearing wasn't a charity garment provided by the hospital, but an exquisite thing, lavishly embroidered, with its own matching bed

36

jacket. She had been given a private room, the staff couldn't be more attentive had she been royalty, and every day gifts of fruit and flowers arrived.

Enrique Ruiz told her that Carlos would be collecting her to bring her home the day after tomorrow. She felt like a cat on a ledge. Trapped.

*　　　*　　　*

She was roused and given the clothes she would need for the journey. Her own suitcase had still not come to light in the wreckage. Her conversation with the señor had been heeded because, sensitive to her needs, instead of the leg-revealing dress she anticipated, here was a trouser suit in a clear bright orange. Lovely uplifting colour! Someone had a pretty good eye for size, she thought, pleased with the fit. But best of all, the trousers hid the hideous bandage on her leg.

She walked out to meet Carlos with a pronounced limp and averted eyes. He took both her hands and said how wonderful she looked. The matron, Dorcas's special doctor and favourite nurse came to the car to wave them off.

They drove in silence for a while. Dorcas was too shy to do anything but look straight ahead. She pretended total absorption in the scenery, which was indeed compelling. The blue mountains stretched to sombre and lonely heights; in the distance she could see the sea.

'I warned you not to cross fate,' Carlos told her.

'So you did.'

'I hope you have learnt your lesson?'

'I'm not sure that I have. I accept only that I am to be a temporary guest in your house,' Dorcas replied in as cool a tone as her runaway heartbeat would allow. 'It will be a pleasant diversion to idle in luxury for a while.'

Her words were chosen as a form of self-protection and not to annoy him. Nevertheless, he looked intensely annoyed.

'Is that all it means to you?'

Rounding a bend at a speed conducive to heightening temper, but faster than caution permitted, Carlos had to swerve violently to avoid an old man, a *campesino*, sitting on top of a cart drawn by a slow, fat donkey. Gathering speed again, mercifully he seemed to have forgotten asking that difficult question.

'Did you eat any breakfast?'

'No.' She had been too tense to eat.

'In that case, we'll stop for something. The drive might prove tiring for you. We mustn't forget this is your first full day out of bed. A breakfast stop will split the journey.'

'Lovely. I'm hungry now.'

Dorcas assumed that Carlos meant to stop at some roadside eating place that happened to be on their way. He proved her assumption

38

wrong by twisting sharply off the main highway. The powerful car began to climb a hazardous mountain road. She felt no qualms, but admired Carlos's prowess behind the wheel. She was content to put her life in his strong, competent hands. Memory overwhelmed her and she was back in hospital again as she remembered reaching out her fingers and having her tentative search met with an answering and reassuring grip.

'That is our quarry,' said Carlos, pointing to a house perched like an eyrie on the edge of a gigantic cliff rising sheer from the sea.

'Who on earth chooses to live there?' she said, pulling out of her reverie to gasp in astonishment.

'My grandmother,' he said. And then with laughing indulgence: 'That isn't the signal to fuss your fingers through your hair. You look charmingly wind blown.'

'Charming!'

Hurriedly she reached into her handbag for her comb. Her handbag had been looped over her arm and had escaped with a scruffed strap and minor scratches. Providence had been on her side in that it was large enough to contain, besides her money and travellers' cheques, make-up and such, her grandmother's bible. Sliding her comb back, her fingers brushed against the bible in comfort.

The road continued to climb and wind, giving occasional breathtaking glimpses of the sea directly below. Dorcas was spellbound by it all. So much so that she lost some of her fear of meeting Carlos's grandmother.

She got out of the car to the realization that she had never touched such heights or feasted her eyes on such peace and beauty. Mountains swept like soaring eagles down to bays of fine white sand; or rounded, less fiercely, to merge with sea and sky. Carlos had to take her arm and drag her away.

'It won't go away. It will be here for you to look at later. Right now, I am impatient for you to meet my grandmother.'

She was infected by his mood. This was important to him. Why? Because . . .? But the answer she provided for herself was one step beyond belief.

Nothing was quite real. Even the view had an illusory quality about it. It was too dramatically drawn to be real.

Then Dorcas was being guided through a door that was far too stout to be an illusion. The hall was wood-panelled, but not sombre. The mellowed simplicity of the dark furniture blended well with the softly-hued fabrics of the pretty patchwork cushions and throw-over covers.

A Spanish woman came forward to greet them. Carlos introduced her as Inez, his grandmother's maid-companion. Inez went to inform her mistress; Carlos sent Dorcas a look that was meant to inspire confidence. It did.

40

But this given courage was immediately lost in awe of meeting his grandmother.

Doña Madelena was a tiny, graceful, imperious figure, despite the fact that the tapping, silver-topped stick was a necessary walking aid, and not for effect. Her face was like a cameo; silver hair peeped from beneath an exquisite lace shawl. Eyes, undimmed by age, rested on Carlos first, as if there was a great hunger in her to see her beloved grandson. Satisfied that he was in fine health and humour, she turned to Dorcas.

She held out both her hands. 'So this is the young lady I have been hearing so much about. Quite the heroine, aren't you?'

Dorcas didn't dare take her hands away until she felt the gentle dismissal in the old señora's fingers. And then she put her hands demurely to her sides and tried not to look embarrassed or coy. Very difficult in view of her tingling fingertips and warm cheeks.

'Dorcas doesn't like talking about it,' Carlos said drily.

'And quite right, too,' applauded his grandmother. 'Can't abide people who make capital of a moment's glory. Not that I'm minimizing yours, child. It was a brave thing you did, and now we will forget about it.' Turning to Carlos she said briskly: 'How long are you here for?'

'For breakfast, *abuela*. Dorcas didn't eat any at the hospital and she's fading away.'

41

'And I suppose you will eat merely to keep Dorcas company?'

'Of course. I have been brought up to be polite.'

Breakfast consisted of fruit juice, morning baked rolls, honey, a peach preserve, and endless cups of coffee with a taste that lived up to its heavenly aroma.

Doña Madelena scraped back her chair and braced herself for the slow and difficult task of forcing her rheumaticky legs to rise. Carlos stepped forward, diffidently offering assistance which was accepted with alacrity.

'I am not as fiercely independent these days. The infirmities of age have an oddly humbling effect.'

The thought of anything humbling this wonderful old lady brought a lump to Dorcas's throat.

'And now, Carlos, you may disappear for the next hour. I am going to conduct Dorcas on a tour of the house. I know she is only just out of hospital—' Answering her grandson's look— 'I promise not to overtax her strength. A snail could keep up with my pace.' Her chin swept autocratically high. 'Dorcas, your arm!'

Dorcas gave it. She thought they must look a comical pair as they limped off together.

Doña Madelena's desire to show Dorcas the house was an excuse. She wanted to talk to Dorcas without her grandson's hampering presence, and it was easier to do that while ostensibly otherwise occupied.

Dorcas was absently fingering a beautiful tapestry, when a voice said in her ear: 'All this will be my grandson's one day. This house is too big for me and I shall welcome moving into a smaller establishment. When Carlos marries he will bring his bride to this eagle-flighted fortress.'

Dorcas countered: 'Isabel will be a very lucky girl. I will think of her in her mountainside home, surrounded by so many beautiful things, when I am back in cold, rain-splashed England.'

'So you know about Isabel! I like you, Dorcas. I like the polite way you put an interfering old woman in her place. I've always spoken my mind, and few have dared to answer back. Isabel Roca is not right for my grandson. I can reduce Isabel to a shivering heap with just one look.'

'How barbarous!' said Dorcas, forgetting herself.

Her rash reply did not cause offence, and even tempted a slight smile.

'It is our heritage. We have been captured by barbarians so many times that this streak of cruelty runs in our blood. Do you like my grandson?'

'You have a fine collection of porcelain, señora,' Dorcas said, pointedly turning the subject.

*   *   *

It was time for them to leave. Doña Madelena told Dorcas: 'You must come and see me again, child.'

'I would like that.' Dorcas kissed a cheek that was surprisingly smooth, with little hope that she would be able to keep her promise.

'It will be,' said the old señora, confidently squeezing Dorcas's fingers.

*   *   *

'You made a hit with Grandmother,' said Carlos, when they were on their way.

'Yes.' Dorcas surreptitiously wiped a tear away with her fingers. It had worked both ways. Carlos's grandmother had made a hit with her.

'I admire the way you stood up to her. People have been known to faint when she fixes them with that eye of hers. She is a barbed-tongued old aristocrat with a dash of the devil in her soul.'

'Carlos Ruiz, that's a horrid thing to say and totally untrue. You don't deserve such a dear, sweet, kind . . .' She stopped. The adjectives didn't fit. But that wasn't her main reason for breaking off. A thought had just struck her. She took it up.

'You must have been listening. I only stood up to your grandmother once, and that was

44

during a supposedly private conversation. When you were with us, my conduct was exemplary.'

'If you must know, Grandmother told me.' There was an essence of teasing in his smile. 'She said, "Yes, my grandson, you were right"'

Dorcas frowned. There wasn't another remark he could have flung at her so guaranteed to pique her curiosity. He's daring me to ask him to explain, she thought. Well I won't give him the satisfaction of knowing that I'm curious to my toenails. She averted her chin from the mocking speculation of his gaze.

He pulled the car into the side of the road and switched off the engine. He then turned her face with his hand. 'I shouldn't spar with you, however much I enjoy it. Not while you are still so weak. I'm taking an unfair advantage.'

'Men do,' she said.

'What do you know about men?'

He took both her hands in his. The conciliatory gesture dampened the fire of her anger, and stoked up another fire. 'Enough.' She modified: 'Enough to put me on my guard now.'

She could not stay annoyed with Carlos while her hands were cherished within his, neither could she stop the pulse in her wrist responding to his touch. He held her hands captive, but it was her heart she feared for.

In her awkwardness and confusion, the

45

words she never meant to say leapt impetuously from her tongue. 'What did you say about me to your grandmother that made her reply the way she did?'

He threw back his head and laughed. 'If you really want to know, I told my grandmother that she would meet her match in you. She told me I was right. Would you like to know what she said to me after that?'

'Not really.'

'I'm going to tell you, just the same. She told me that I too had met my match.'

'What a silly thing to say.'

'Wasn't it,' he said annoyingly. 'But then, women do say silly things.'

'Of course, you have a vast knowledge of women.'

'Enough,' he said, without modification.

Dorcas sat up very straight. After a pause, long enough to accommodate a mental count of ten, she said: 'There is something I would like to make absolutely clear.'

'Yes?' He looked more amused than apprehensive.

'I am not returning with you voluntarily to your home. Circumstance has put me in the invidious position of having no alternative.' And don't you dare laugh at that, she thought, clenching and unclenching her taut fingers.

He did not laugh. On the contrary, a frown shuttered his expression. 'I am sorry you find it so painful. It does not please me to bend you

46

against your will. That is the last thing I would want to do.'

Just before he closed his eyes, as if the bright light pained him, Dorcas saw a look there she had never seen before. Tenderness? Perhaps. And something else she did not dare to analyse. Up to that moment she had been in full control of herself. To her disgust, his glance slit through her resolve to expose her vulnerability. She was glad he closed his eyes. He could not see that her hands were trembling and that her eyes were filled with tears.

She knew she had said it all wrong. She was prickly and gauche in the ways of men. Her grandmother had frequently told her she was an awkward girl, completely without charm. 'You should take a leaf out of Michael's book,' Dorcas had been told on countless occasions. But Michael had influenced by flattery and bewitched by whatever flowery falsehood he could lay his tongue to. If this was charm, then she wanted no part of it. She did not regret not having her brother's false tongue, but in that misunderstood and painful silence, she wished she possessed the gift of simple eloquence.

They ate the picnic lunch Carlos's grandmother had thoughtfully provided. Conversation was desultory, and the food stuck in Dorcas's throat.

'I did not mean to sound ungracious,' she said. 'I'm sorry.'

'I know. It's all right, Dorcas.'

He lingered over saying her name. Without looking at his face she knew his expression had softened towards her.

'It's just that . . .' She shrugged helplessly. It was blissfully clear in her head. She knew what she wanted to say, but the words would not form. She had apologized. He had accepted her apology. It would have to stand at that.

'Come,' said Carlos at length. 'We should make a move.' This time, instead of unlawfully entering the curly wrought-iron gates, her suitcase bumping against her legs, she arrived at the Villa Serena, an honoured and welcome guest.

Enrique Ruiz came down the terrace steps to greet her. His beard brushed the back of her hand, and his eyes spoke a welcome before the extravagant words fell from his lips. 'My house is your house. Come.'

He took her arm to guide her up the steps to where his wife stood, one hand-made shoe of grey suede tapping the blue-grey tiles.

'Welcome to Villa Serena,' said Rose Ruiz. Although her greeting was as warm as her husband's, Dorcas sensed, because it wasn't apparent to the ear, a holding back. The eyes briefly transferred to her son had clouded depths. Yet nothing clouded the compassion in her voice as she said: 'You look tired, Dorcas. The drive has stolen the colour from your cheeks.' Rose Ruiz continued to talk, making

48

comforting, welcoming noises that melted into the ice of Dorcas's reserve. Dorcas disclosed, on kindly probing, that they had eaten, but yes she would love a cup of tea. The conversation was conducted in English, but a cup of tea said welcome in any language.

The tea was served with cakes and pastries. To be polite, Dorcas selected a biscuit which left a lingering taste of honey in her mouth. There was an underlying taste, a tangy sharpness that Dorcas could not make out. And it was the same with Rose Ruiz's manner. She was very sweet . . . and yet.

Carlos was talking now. In making a point, his hand came to rest, not sensually but in friendly familiarity, on Dorcas's shoulder. She had a sudden craving to turn her cheek into his hand. Her shoulder and his hand were in delicious harmony and she wanted to draw in every last drop of comfort.

A teacup rattled against a saucer. Rose Ruiz's eyes were concentrated on her in a look of such fixed intensity that Dorcas's cheeks turned pink. Something jumped between them. Rose Ruiz set her cup down. Her fingers shook and Dorcas saw that she had splashed some tea on her skirt.

'Would you like to rest in your room before dinner, Dorcas?' The slight edge in her voice did not deprive it of kindness and nobody but Dorcas seemed to notice her agitation.

Dorcas replied gratefully: 'I would, please.

How kind of you to know.' Still dwelling on the thought of kindness, she said: 'Thank you for providing me with these lovely clothes. I seem to be causing a great deal of trouble.'

Before Rose Ruiz could make the appropriate answer, Enrique Ruiz stepped in to say: 'You could never be a trouble, my dear. As for the suit you are wearing, I'm not sure whom I should compliment. My wife for having the good taste to choose it, or yourself for looking so attractive in it.'

'Anyone would look attractive in this suit,' Dorcas replied sedately.

'You are too modest, Dorcas,' Rose Ruiz told her. 'I did not choose that suit. Carlos did,' she admitted, forestalling the question on Dorcas's lips.

'Did you?' said Dorcas, her eyes swinging back to Carlos in surprise.

The spontaneity of her delight found its twin in his eye. And more. The warmth she read smoothed out her nervously twisting fingers. It wrapped her in sympathetic understanding and made it easy for her to sparkle a big 'Thank you' up at him.

His return smile encompassed his gratification. She felt a deep wave of relief because they were still friends. Deeper friends than they would normally have been because of his vigil by her bed in hospital. Something stirred in her memory, but it slid away again as Rose Ruiz said:

50

'If you are ready, Dorcas?'

As Rose Ruiz conducted her to her room, Dorcas managed to look around. The feeling was of space and tranquillity. A predominance of white walls and grey-blue floors. Occasional touches of old gold and rose pink, with the odd splash of crimson. Restful, but not dull. The residence of a Spanish gentleman only lightly influenced by his English bride. Don Enrique's English Rose had obviously slotted into the Spanish way of life and had not tried to imprint her own strong personality, at least not on any of the public rooms.

Even though Dorcas was dragging her feet with tiredness, she had to stop for entrancing seconds to admire the beauty of a mosaic floor, and to let her eye climb a pillar to a frieze depicting chivalrous deeds from the pages of Spain's long and turbulent history. The wide, cool hall was hung with tapestries showing scenes from Don Quixote; in the courtyard beyond, water from a fountain splashed into a smooth marble basin.

A finely scrolled staircase led to a gallery where family portraits looked down at Dorcas with haughty expressions and living eyes. At least three were obviously by the hand of the same painter. He had put on canvas not only the features but the characters of his subjects. Or so it seemed to Dorcas. Here and there were paintings of notable scenes and places by famous Spanish painters. She thought she spotted a Velázquez. Another painting had the harsh colouring and distortion of shapes in the style of El Greco. There was time to be spent here in pleasant discovery. But later. Now she was being shown into the room that was to be hers.

Once again the walls were white to complement the rich dark wood of the furniture, which was almost the colour of purple grapes. A *vargueño* stood in the corner, its two doors hung vertically and it stood on bun feet. Crimson rugs splashed the floor, resembling giant paeony heads.

Rose Ruiz adjusted the shutters to show Dorcas the birdcage balcony. And, crossing the room again, opened a door to reveal the luxury of a private bathroom.

'I think you will be comfortable,' she said in amazing understatement. It looked like heaven to Dorcas. 'When you have rested, I will send Teresa along to introduce herself. She is very young, but during the time she has been with us she has acquitted herself well. She will look after you nicely.'

'Thank you, señora.'

Rose Ruiz inclined her handsome head and her lips closed on a gentle smile. 'Later we will talk.' She adjusted the shutters again so that the light filtered meagrely into the room.

Dorcas took off her trouser suit and watched her hostess hang it in the wardrobe. It looked very forlorn, all by itself. Forlorn was how Dorcas felt as she crept into bed. Bewildered, used up—no reserves of strength left to carry her through an uncertain future.

Rose Ruiz went. Dorcas slept. To dream.

In her dream she was walking in the gallery, beneath the stately portraits of the long-dead Ruizs. Steely fingers thrust themselves out of the frames, and the picture people passed her from one to the other, hustling her down the stairs and through the stout outer door which slammed shut with such a violent bang that Dorcas woke up. She was trembling and her sleep-flushed cheeks were wet with tears.

'Oh, señorita! The wind got behind the door and made it bang. I'm sorry. I did not mean to wake you.' Two frightened eyes peeped at Dorcas. 'The señorita's clothes have just arrived and I thought I might very quietly steal in and unpack them as a surprise for when the señorita woke up. Only . . .'

'My clothes!' said Dorcas, at once vitally awake. 'You mean my suitcase has been recovered, Teresa? It is Teresa, isn't it?'

The little maid blinked back her surprise that she wasn't going to be scolded for waking her mistress, and bobbed a curtsy that nearly sent the boxes in her arms toppling to the floor.

Dorcas's knowledge of Spanish was not good enough to take in every word, but she managed to get the gist of what Teresa was saying. Her suitcase had been pronounced

53

irretrievably lost in the wreckage. The clothes, in their fine boxes, had been ordered from an exclusive fashion shop in Madrid.

Dorcas caught the top box and pulled off the lid. 'Oh, Teresa, look!' she said, reverently lifting a floor-length dress in a deep orchid pink with billowy sleeves cut to flow from the waist. 'Have you ever seen anything as lovely?' she said ecstatically.

'*Si*, señorita, this,' said the little Spanish maid, peering into a second box at a misty blue, evening trouser suit.

The discarded tissue-paper was tossed carelessly aside until the floor was floating in filmy sheets of pink and blue and white that settled like giant-sized confetti. The two girls, as happy as larks in full song, exclaimed and gasped and twittered delightedly until the last box was unpacked and the wardrobe and drawers housed all these exciting garments.

She'd never had this many new clothes at once, not even after a childish growing spurt when her dresses strained across her chest and crept up her leg. Her mother had taken her shopping and bought her a whole new wardrobe, including ballet shoes, because in the golden days before her parents died it had been her ambition to be a ballerina. She had the build. The small head and the graceful, well-set neck; strong straight legs and well-arched feet. She kept up her dancing, after the untimely death of her parents, but by this time

54

she knew she lacked the star quality to reach the top. She could laugh now at the supreme egotism of her long-ago dream. There were too many things she hadn't taken into consideration; the fierce competition, her lack of ruthlessness, the tug of family commitments.

When her big break came, she hadn't been able to take it. A rather important man had come to see her backstage at the theatre within thirty minutes walk of her grand-mother's home. Bluntly he told her, 'In my opinion you'll never achieve star status, but your talent is wasted here. I'm taking my company on tour next month. There's an opening for you if you're interested.'

Dorcas was interested. She knew that he had paid her a tremendous compliment. But the timing was wrong. Her grandmother's health was beginning to fail. It wasn't until she thought about leaving that Dorcas realized how much her grandmother had come to rely on her. She had no alternative but to turn the offer down.

All that, of course, was in the past. She must put any hopes firmly behind her, now that she did not possess two strong legs. She probably wouldn't have made the grade, anyway.

She didn't feel bitter, because it wasn't in her nature to harbour acrimonious thoughts, just sad, nostalgic perhaps. She was glad her suitcase was lost in the wreckage because in it were the ballet shoes she never went anywhere without. At least she didn't have them staring her in the face as a painful reminder.

CHAPTER THREE

Next day, even before Dorcas had breakfasted, the nurse came to dress her leg. Her name was Anita. Olive complexioned, dark hair tied back to give a neat, workmanlike appearance, she had a pert, pretty face and a fresh, engaging manner.

'Well now,' she said, examining the long cut which in turn had caused severe bruising to the muscle. 'That's what I call a very tidy job. You had a good surgeon, señorita. Your healthy skin will soon heal this up. See how neatly it is knitting together. That slight redness there is your army of corpuscles fighting off the infection. I will dress your leg now. Very soon I hope to leave the bandage off.' She worked as she spoke; her movements had the same brisk efficiency as her mode of speech. When she had finished she gave Dorcas's leg a little pat. 'There you are.' She rocked back on her heels and surveyed Dorcas with wide, serious eyes. 'You do know, don't you, that had the injury been a fraction to the left, had the cut been say about here, you would have sustained more than a bruised muscle and could have permanently lost the use of your leg? I hope you realize what a lucky girl you are.'

'Yes,' said Dorcas, suitably sober, 'I know I am a very lucky girl.'

'I want you to use that leg,' the little nurse instructed, 'but I don't want you to abuse it. By that I mean take only gentle exercise and rest it the moment it feels tired. If your leg suddenly gives way and lets you down, don't worry, it's only the muscle objecting to what's happening to it. The sooner we get the bandage off the better, and then we can get you into that splendid swimming pool out there.' She smiled, picked up her capacious bag and said: '*Adiós. Hasta la vista.*'

Dorcas echoed the goodbye, then wandered out to the patio overlooking the swimming pool. A maid, older than her own Teresa, but with the same dark eyes and shy demeanour, appeared to ask her if she would like her breakfast served on the patio.

'Is it usual?' said Dorcas, before she noticed the table there for apparently just that purpose, complete with the remains of somebody's breakfast which had not yet been cleared away.

'*Sí*, señorita—' Stacking the pretty breakfast service with painstaking care '—The young señor prefers to take his breakfast on the patio.'

Dorcas touched a coffee pot that was still warm to the fingers. 'I suppose don Carlos has left for work?'

'*Sí*, señorita.' The maid added the coffee pot to the things on the tray. 'I will bring the señorita's breakfast at once. Has the señorita

58

any preference?'

'No. How are you called?'

'Brigida, señorita'

'Then, Brigida, just bring me fruit juice, rolls and preserve—any kind. Oh, and coffee please.'

'*Sí*, señorita.' Brigida's taut features warmed into a shy smile. She returned with Dorcas's breakfast in express time.

As Dorcas ate the flaky, crusty rolls to the aroma of perfect coffee, she felt deliciously lazy, pleasantly unrushed. She couldn't help comparing this feeling of relaxed content with her past rushed existence.

About this time she would have been staring at some ghastly patterned wallpaper, choking down toast, in all probability after its burnt edges had been scraped in the kitchen sink because she didn't seem to have the knack of choosing landladies who could achieve even an elementary stage of cooking. And then, after gulping down a cup of weak coffee, or worse— stewed tea—she would dash off to a day dedicated to strenuous dance routines. She wondered if it was wicked of her not to regret overmuch what had happened.

The dancing that had been her very life, and which she thought would always be her first passion, was already fading into insignificance. She dare not admit to herself that Carlos was responsible for this.

'You've had breakfast?'

Dorcas looked up to see the slight elevation of Rose Ruiz's exquisitely shaped eyebrows.

Dorcas said she had.

'A second cup of coffee, perhaps? To keep me company?'

'It will be my third,' said Dorcas in acceptance.

Brigida brought a fresh pot of coffee. Rose Ruiz poured out two cups, placing one in front of Dorcas.

Dorcas lifted her cup as a child might, hoping her fingers would not disgrace her. Charming as her hostess was, there was still that something indefinable in her manner that made Dorcas feel nervous.

Yet no eyes could have been kinder as their owner enquired: 'Did you sleep well?'

'I had a wonderful night's sleep, thank you. And I love the room you have given me.'

'I am so pleased. And Teresa? Do you find her compatible?'

'Oh yes! Teresa and I are friends already. I feel spoilt having her. You must know I'm not used to having my own personal maid.'

'A little spoiling does nobody any harm. You are a natural target for a bit of cosseting. You have a charming lack of avarice that makes giving a pleasure. It isn't in your nature to covet what is someone else's.'

Dorcas had the feeling that this was not idle flattery. The sweet talk was leading up to something specific, something less sweet.

Irrelevantly she noticed that Rose Ruiz's lipstick and nail varnish were the same pearly shade. It made her want to fold her own unvarnished nails into the palms of her hands. When she looked they were already there.

'If there is anything you want, Dorcas, don't hesitate to ask. Try to look upon this as your home, if you can. Make free use of any of the rooms. If you're a reader, you'll find a fair selection of books in English. Carlos, especially, regretted not being able to take today off to keep you company. But, well, it's not so easy at the moment. My husband's business, like that of his friend's, Alfonso Roca's, is a small fish being eaten by the sharks. It is, I believe, a world-wide problem.'

'We certainly have it in England. The larger competitive companies are swallowing the small family concerns.'

'And what do the small fish, the family concerns, do to combat the sharks?'

'They join forces.'

'That is precisely what my husband and don Alfonso are considering; in fact the details of the merger are under discussion. It would be a great pity if something unforeseen were to happen to prevent it taking place.' Midnight-blue eyes steadied on sherry-gold ones. Dorcas found herself holding her breath on the knowledge that the point of the conversation was soon to be explained to her. 'Looking to the future, when my Enrique and don Alfonso retire, because don Alfonso has no son of his own, Carlos will be in full control.'

Dorcas saw what Rose Ruiz was getting at.

'Don Alfonso cannot be expected to agree to the merger unless he is certain in his mind that his daughter's interest will be safeguarded. It is both a blessing and a relief that Isabel and Carlos find each other *simpático.*'

'Are you saying their engagement is a major clause of the merger?' Dorcas managed.

'No, I'm not saying that. It's pretty obvious, though, that don Alfonso will feel happier about handing over the running of the business to Carlos if he's his son-in-law.'

Dorcas's heartbeats seemed to fill her ears as her mouth moved to ask: 'What does Carlos think about this?'

'I can assure you that Carlos is not the sacrificial lamb,' Rose Ruiz replied on a small, wry smile. 'It is true that Carlos has not admitted to himself that he could love Isabel yet. Any problem there is of a purely temporary nature. The realization of love takes many forms. It can erupt like a sunburst—and risk burning itself out on its own intensity. By far the best sort of love creeps up so gradually that it is difficult to pinpoint the exact moment it entered the relationship. That is how it will be for Carlos and Isabel. Carlos has known Isabel since she was a child, and still regards her as such. He taught her to swim, alongside his sister, even regarded her as a second sister. But Isabel is not his sister and she has reached an age when he could teach her other things, and learn something himself in the process. If he played at love with her, before long he would come to love her. Isabel is a sweet girl. It would be no hardship.'

It occurred to Dorcas that Rose Ruiz wasn't just explaining the set-up, but warning her off. She obviously saw Dorcas as a threat. She had taken a hand-to-shoulder contact and an exchange of glances and exaggerated it in her mind.

Dorcas didn't believe that Carlos's marriage to Isabel Roca was as cut and dried as his mother was making out. It was a possibility—no more and no less—in no way threatened by Dorcas's presence.

Rose Ruiz stressed: 'It will be a good marriage. Isabel has been brought up to accept the fact that Spain is a masculine country. She will expect Carlos to dominate the marriage. It wouldn't do for you, Dorcas. I have never found marriage to a dominant man stifling, for the simple reason that prior to my marriage I'd never tasted this so-called freedom and equality of the sexes. We didn't have it in my day. You don't miss what you've never had. What you know isn't always best, but it's safer to stick to it.'

Meaning I should stick to what I know best,

63

thought Dorcas.

'The independence we enjoy now has been too hard-won to be lightly thrown away,' Dorcas agreed, allowing that as a point in Rose Ruiz's favour. 'I enjoy the liberty that, for example, has allowed me to travel abroad on my own. I can't see myself ever accepting the passive role in marriage. I would want to be an equal.'

'Equality is a hard pendulum to set,' Rose Ruiz replied with undeniable truth.

Dorcas nodded. 'I know what you mean. In America it has gone the other way. The women there dominate the marriage. And that's no good either. If one is aware of the danger . . . surely . . . ?' She didn't really expect a reply to her half formed question. On the other hand she did not expect such an abrupt, laughably transparent twist to the conversation.

'I must invite the Rocas over for dinner. Soon.'

Dorcas felt a moment's pity for her. She still doesn't know, she thought. Carlos was her son. A son is a person of the highest ideals. As well as being a son, Carlos was also a man. He looked at Dorcas with a man's eyes, and liked what he saw. Perhaps he even wanted to do more than look. It didn't mean he wanted to marry her.

Dorcas thought she had made a fair job of the evaluation, until she remembered she hadn't accounted for the blanks. The earlier part of her stay in hospital, while she was under heavy sedation, was a blank. People had come and gone, but Carlos had stayed by her bed. She experienced an impression of closeness that came in almost remembering. Trying to clarify her thoughts was like trying to feel through glass. Splinters of memory pierced her awareness, but not enough to piece together to make a whole.

*   *   *

That evening, at dinner, Dorcas did not feel hungry. The soup went down very slowly. The fish left on her plate was an insult to the cook. She couldn't face the pot-roast of veal.

Enrique Ruiz leaned forward to rap her knuckles in a proprietorial gesture, establishing her entry into the bosom of the family by reproof. One did not upbraid a guest.

'Why are you not eating?' He spoke like a father addressing a much-loved but tiresome daughter. His eyes were kindly and concerned.

'I am not hungry.' Dorcas looked squarely at him. She thought she had never liked anyone more, except of course, Carlos. To please him she would eat up every spoonful of her dessert. But oh! how pleased she would be when the meal was over and she could go to her room. She needed to come to terms with her thoughts.

The level of the wine carafe was considerably lower; the coffee cups were empty. At last she could say: 'I am rather tired. Will you excuse me, please?'

Enrique Ruiz smiled, and once again his smile was almost a hug. *'Yes, niña.* Your eyes grow small in your head. Goodnight. Sleep well, my dear.'

'Shall I come with you?' said Rose Ruiz.

It didn't seem an odd notion for the señora to accompany her to her room and perhaps tuck her in bed. Nevertheless, Dorcas said in a sleepy voice: 'Please do not trouble. I can find my own way.'

'As you wish. Goodnight, Dorcas.'

'Goodnight señora, señor.' Before she could add his name, Carlos had risen from his chair and his hand was supporting her elbow.

'I will see you to your room.'

The moment they were on the other side of the dining-room door, he said: 'Even as tired as you are, a breath of air will prove beneficial before you turn in. Come out into the garden for just a little while.'

There was an element of self-punishment in saying yes, but Dorcas did not have the will to turn down the invitation.

In the blue-mink sky, every star had come out of hiding. She stroked her bare arms and said, because she felt the need to fill the dangerous silence with meaningless chatter,

66

'How delicious to feel so warm so late in the evening. At home I would have had to cover up my arms, muffle up even.'

Carlos's eyes regarded her indulgently. 'Chatter if you like. If it makes you feel less nervous of me.'

'Why should I feel nervous of you?'

'Oh Dorcas, that look. You put your head on one side. So. It looks very chic and provocative, but it's not that at all. You do it when you are uncertain, not quite in command of the situation. I am beginning to understand you a little. I thought that endearing naivety was deliberately contrived. Only it isn't, is it Dorcas?'

'Since you know it all . . .' She was going to say, 'there is little more I can add, and as I really am tired, I'll say goodnight.'

Carlos's: 'I know what you are going to say,' cut her off.

'Then please tell me.'

'You can hardly keep your eyes open. You want to go to your bed and sleep for a week.' The stiffening of her body told him that in essence he'd got it right. 'Do you always run away from things that—' Slight pause— 'perplex you?'

Run away? Did she? Because she lacked the courage to follow up her impulses.

'Why are you so jumpy? Is it me, or are you always like this when you are alone with a man? We aren't all alike, you know.'

67

'What's that supposed to mean?'

'It means I can't make up my mind about you. You've either had a disastrous experience . . . or no experience at all.'

'I'm not going to challenge you to guess which,' she said huskily.

'See what I mean? That's either a provocative response, or a naive one.'

He put his hand up and combed his fingers through his hair in a sort of reflex action that accentuated his puzzlement and made him look oddly vulnerable. She knew an overriding impulse to raise her own hand and allow it to follow the course his had taken.

And then she wasn't thinking it, she was in the process of doing it. His hand was there to ambush hers, trapping her fingers against his cheek as he eased her forward. Not to kiss her; to hold her. It was a nursery embrace, tender as any he could have given his tiny niece. Yet little Rosita's spine would not have tingled at the encounter. Rosita might have felt safe and warm though, and let her head drop . . . just so . . . against his broad chest.

'You're not playing this one fair.'

He didn't need to tell her that. Even as he held her so lightly, she could sense his inner struggle not to crush her close. It was delicious to feel safe in his arms—knowing she wasn't.

In bed, just before sleep put in its drowsy claim, her mind drifted on bitter-sweet thought. It was this sort of madness Rose Ruiz,

68

so kindly intentioned, had warned her off. There was no permanent place in Carlos's life for her. She was risking her heart for his temporary amusement. Perhaps this new dalliance would make him resist the pressures for a while longer, but in the end the interests of the family business would come first and Carlos would accept his . . . the word that boomeranged to mind mocked her . . . fate.

The days passed, one melting sweetly into the next, without turning up any event of great significance. To her surprise, Dorcas found she had made a friend in Rose Ruiz. Although she often looked at her with tucks in her forehead, on the whole she seemed glad of the company Dorcas provided.

The dressing was removed from her leg. A physiotherapist was engaged and Dorcas dutifully did the exercises she was given. She made certain that she only went in the swimming pool when she was confident of not being seen. She was conscious of the ugliness of the scar, which seemed to be taking its time in fading. For this reason she never wore shorts or short skirts, but settled for jeans and sun-tops during the day, and every evening she blessed fashion for long skirts and trouser suits.

One lunchtime as Dorcas was enjoying her garlic flavoured, fried baby eels seasoned with hot peppers, Rose Ruiz announced without warning: 'The Rocas are dining with us this evening.'

The hotness searing her throat was because of the peppers, Dorcas told herself. She was glad she was going to meet Isabel Roca, if only to appease her morbid curiosity!

She dressed for the event with a chill, premonitory excitement, selecting her prettiest dress, a fine silky lawn in an ethereal shade of green. The beauty of the dress was in the generously full sleeves, caught in lavishly embroidered wristbands. The fragile green of the dress enhanced her hair to a silken fairness, but it stole the colour from her cheeks. Perhaps it was not a good choice at that. It made her look younger and more vulnerable than her twenty-two years.

A knock sounded on her door and in answer to her: '*Adelante*,' the man who was never far from her thoughts entered her room.

She was startled. She had thought it would be Teresa or one of the other maids. It was the first time Carlos had been to her room. In a strict Spanish household, it was slightly improper.

'I've come to fetch you. Are you ready?'

'Almost. Will I do?' she asked impulsively.

He smiled at her need to ask for his assurance. 'You look charming.' Simply said with sincerity. More touching than the most extravagant compliment. 'Although—a little pale.'

'I have still to colour my lips.'

70

She picked up her lipstick, but before she could apply it to her mouth, he planted a kiss there.

'That was a very arrogant thing to do,' she protested.

'I am an arrogant Spaniard. You, in keeping with most English women, are not naturally subservient, but I will make allowances. Ah . . . the effect is achieved. But I will never know whether it was my kiss, or temper that has brought the colour to your cheeks.'

Dorcas could not think of a thing to say to that.

'Come.' He propelled her by the arm. 'Let us go. Our guests will be arriving at any moment and it will be discourteous if we are not with my parents to greet them.'

They walked down the stairs. From their baroque frames, the long-dead Ruizs looked down on Dorcas, their painted features impervious to the state of her mind. Not so the man at her side. Carlos knew, not only how to, but that he had tied her emotions in knots. The effects of this most recent emotional skirmish with him coalesced with her anticipatory dread at meeting Isabel Roca.

'You look like a little girl in mortal trepidation of her first grown-up party,' Carlos said perceptively.

'I wish you hadn't said that. I was hoping it didn't show. I wore green then.'

'When?'

'At my first grown-up party. I can remember it all so clearly. I wouldn't let go of my brother Michael's hand. He became very annoyed.'

'I would have found your shyness rather touching.'

'Not if you were several years older and didn't want a small nuisance around, upsetting your plans and cramping your style.'

'I am several years older.' He stopped walking and automatically so did she. 'You *are* a small nuisance and you *have* upset my plans. As for the other . . .'

She wondered if he knew what 'cramping the style' meant.

Once again he demonstrated that uncanny and disturbing quality to read her mind. 'My mother is English. Had you forgotten? I have visited England, staying with my English relatives, often enough to have picked up the idiom. And so I repeat, as for the other, that too. You have most decidedly cramped my style. In all fairness, perhaps not you, but the circumstances of your enforced stay. You have not fully recovered from your ordeal. Not only did your leg sustain injuries, but your emotions have been badly shaken up. It does not help that you are alone, in a strange country. All these things combine to create a false picture. Propinquity, gratitude, both have chameleon qualities that are all too easy to mistake. It will be better when you are not so alone, when your brother arrives.'

72

'M-my brother?' Dorcas, who had never stuttered in her life, did so now. 'Michael's on holiday s-somewhere in France. Why should he come here?' Nothing he could have said could have deflated her more.

'Why do you look so surprised? You know we are trying to locate your brother.'

'I thought you'd given up. Obviously he isn't proving easy to find and . . .'

'You must think I give up very easily.' His tone was both remonstrative and teasing, and of the two it was the latter which disturbed her most.

'It's not that at all. I wasn't questioning your persistency. I'm quite sure that whatever you set your mind to is accomplished with . . .' Her voice finished on a high, incomplete note.

'Ruthless determination?' he suggested, supplying a possible ending. 'Or would "by fair means or foul" be more what you had in mind?'

'No it would not,' she replied with spirit. 'I don't hold such a low opinion of you.'

His breath released slowly. 'I'm pleased to hear it,' he said on a bland smile.

Dorcas wished she had something to smile about. She hoped Carlos never managed to trace her brother. She didn't want Michael here.

CHAPTER FOUR

They had lingered too long. The Señores *de* Roca had already arrived by the time Dorcas and Carlos stepped down into the hall.

Dorcas was barely aware of the grey-haired *caballero* and his comely spouse. This, even though her eyes had to skip past them to reach Isabel who was being warmly greeted by Rose Ruiz. All her impatience achieved was a second glimpse of Isabel's back. As if her memory needed refreshing of that impossibly tiny waist and tightly drawn-back, black hair. Rose Ruiz's watchful eyes met Dorcas's over the top of Isabel's head. Dorcas hadn't realized how tiny Isabel was. She was like a doll.

And then Isabel was swinging away and approaching Carlos in a rustle of stiff crimson silk. She held up a pale, untouched-by-the-sun cheek for his kiss. Not coquettishly, but with the warmth that exists between friends of long-standing.

She turned, slowly. And Dorcas braced up to looking at the most beautiful girl she had ever seen. Her long lashed, black eyes and doll features could take the severe hairstyle; the delicate china complexion looked good above the crimson silk that scooped and contoured her body in the most dramatic way. Dorcas's throat lumped. She couldn't think what Carlos was waiting for. Why didn't he pick Isabel up and rush her to the altar before someone else did?

'So you are Dorcas,' Isabel said, tilting her chin and letting the delight and pleasure flow freely from the bright sincerity of her eyes. She was, apparently, as sweet as she looked. 'I've heard so much about you. And yet you are not at all as I expected.'

Dorcas could have returned that compliment—because it was said in a complimentary sense—neither was Isabel as she expected, despite Rose Ruiz's cautionary words.

'I thought you would be—oh, I don't know—hard and sophisticated. It is not enough to travel on your own, which shows much enterprise, but to have the nerve to do what you did for Feli and Rosita. You risked your own life! I'm quite in awe of you. I should have gone to pieces.'

'You wouldn't,' Dorcas said generously. 'In similar circumstances, you would have done just the same. It was an intuitive reaction. A lucky one too. I'm not brave, and I rarely jump the right way.'

Rose Ruiz entered the conversation. 'Dorcas is a modest heroine.' Her voice was warm with pride. 'Later, you two girls can talk all you want to. Right now, Isabel, I want to introduce Dorcas to your mama and papa. As you know, Dorcas, don Alfonso and doña Maria are the dearest of all our friends.'

Don Alfonso was very correct, very Spanish in his bearing, but not in a way that Dorcas found intimidating. The timidity she always felt when meeting a new face melted under his kindly influence. He spoke to her in English and Dorcas returned the compliment by trying out her Spanish on him. When she said: '*Encantada*,' she truly meant that she was delighted to meet him.

His señora, her dark eyes reflecting his like a second thought, was dressed in the sombre drama of the unrelieved black which Latin ladies of her age group still favoured. It was too harsh for her. Dorcas couldn't help thinking that a less severe silver grey would have been a kinder choice.

The moment the introductions were completed, Carlos offered his apologies for not being at the door when they arrived.

'It is forgotten,' don Alfonso said expansively.

Isabel interrupted, impishly: 'Do not let him off so lightly, Papa. Why were you detained, Carlos? We thought you'd got lost.'

'Not lost.' Carlos's eyes slid between mischief and reflection. 'We might have wandered off the track for a moment, but we weren't lost. Wouldn't you agree, Dorcas?'

Dorcas could neither agree nor disagree. She was temporarily without a voice.

Isabel came out tops by not losing her composure. She even managed a smile as she said: 'We must have a delicious long gossip soon, eh Dorcas? We could—how do you say it? —make the comparison?'

'Compare notes,' Dorcas supplied automatically. 'Er . . . yes. That would be nice,' she finished flatly.

At the table, Dorcas ate from habit, with no sense of enjoyment, although a special meal had been planned for the Rocas' visit. She drank the wine—the pride of don Enrique's cellar—with as little appreciation as if it were vinegar.

Rose Ruiz indicated it was time to leave the men to their cigars and brandy, and the womenfolk got up from the table.

'It's stuffy indoors,' Isabel announced. 'Shall we go out on the terrace?'

'You and Dorcas may,' her mama said. Judging by the look on Isabel's face this was the reply she anticipated. '*Tía* Rose and I are more comfortable where we are. But take your shawl, Isabel. It can come in quite cool at night and you know how easily you catch a chill.'

'Yes, Mama,' Isabel said dutifully. 'I left my shawl in the hall. I will go for it straight away. Is there anything I can get for you, *Tía* Rose? Perhaps you would like me to fetch your embroidery or your fan?'

'No, child,' said Rose Ruiz, smiling fondly. 'I am all set for a nice long gossip with your mama. There is nothing more I could want for.'

Nodding, smiling, Isabel made her escape, whisking Dorcas along with her.

'Let us sit here,' Isabel said, pointing to the chairs on the terrace. Sitting down, she threw her shawl from her shoulders in a gesture that was oddly revealing. She fixed Dorcas with her big ingenuous eyes. 'Do you despise me for humouring Mama and being the oh so obedient daughter, and for fawning over *Tía* Rose?' Without waiting for a reply, she said in self-mitigation: 'It makes Mama feel good and it does me no harm. As for the other—' Her eyes slid down to her lap, then up again, but now they were without expression. 'I'd be silly, surely, not to make the nest as comfortable as possible? I don't see how Carlos and I can escape marrying, and there's no point in being on bad terms with my future mama-in-law.'

Dorcas said weakly: 'Do you want to escape?'

'Not really. Carlos will make me a good husband.'

'But—' Dorcas released her breath on a shocked gasp—'you do not love him.' Statement, not question.

'That is true.' Shrugging her shoulders haughtily. 'This will give me the enormous advantage. Biological attraction is very nice, I suppose, but it does have the disadvantage of dimming one's judgement. I can see Carlos as

78

he really is. Which I would not be able to do if my heart beat for him to the point of divine madness.' And then, answering the disapproving set of Dorcas's mouth: 'It works both ways, you know. Carlos does not love me, and so he will know exactly what he is getting. I will adorn his house quite prettily; I will entertain his guests and give him many fine sons.'

'It sounds a cold formula for a marriage,' Dorcas couldn't help saying. 'All set out, like a contract.'

'Precisely so. Marriage is a contract, surely?'

'I suppose it is. But not one I would wish to enter without love. Isabel, don't you ever yearn to be dazed out of your senses? To feel all aglow and intensely alive, and treasure his every smile as something sacred. To live for him alone, and know you would willingly die for him. Feel giddy and shook-up. All because of . . .' She stopped. She was giving too much away. Not only to Isabel—to herself. Did she really feel this intensely about Carlos?

Daintily and fastidiously, Isabel shrugged her shoulders. 'I would not care to feel that way about my husband. To be so *vulnerable* . . .? No, no, I would not like it at all! I have made a study of the marriages of friends and relations. My observations have told me that it is difficult enough to sew a marriage together. Why add to the complications by being emotionally involved?'

'Marriage is not a patchwork quilt. There is no set templet to work to. You can't measure out the requirements to a calculated size—this square of fidelity is too large so let's snip a bit off—and expect to sew it up to make happiness. Don't do it, Isabel. Can't you see what I'm getting at?'

'I would be stupid not to. You want Carlos for yourself. I can't say that I blame you. He is tall and good looking, and fun to be with. He's kind, and even if he does drive me mad with his teasing, most of the time I feel lucky to have him. He's mine and I'm keeping him. I can't let you have him. I'm sorry. It's true that I don't love him, but he is not repulsive to me, which is something. My parents could have chosen someone old enough to be my father and as fat as a butter-ball. Neither is Carlos too steeped in the old tradition. He will cherish me as a wife, without being irksomely protective.'

He is good to look at and fun to be with. He's kind and considerate, tender and arrogant, and he drives *me* mad with his teasing, but if he were mine I'd feel lucky *all* the time. I would never ask for another thing if I could have Carlos.

Aloud, Dorcas said: 'Your views are too calculated. We're back to the patchwork quilt again. You're not being fair to Carlos.'

'You do not need to feel sorry for Carlos. I will not cheat on what goes on under the patchwork quilt.'

Dorcas felt sick.

'Then you are not being fair to yourself. To close your eyes to love is like closing your eyes and your senses to the beauties of nature. Never to hear a bird sing or smell a flower.'

'Who said anything about closing my eyes to love? Carlos will have his women, and I will have . . .'

'Are you two girls having a pleasant conversation?' The interruption was timely.

Isabel smiled up at Carlos. 'An enlightening one!' she said mischievously. 'Wouldn't you agree, Dorcas?'

'Oh . . . yes!'

'M'm,' said Carlos, his grave eyes acknowledging the touch of atmosphere that still lingered between them.

Did he know they hadn't been chewing on the usual candied girlie gossip, but something with more of a bite to it? If he suspected his name had figured prominently, his self-effacing expression gave no clue.

'Would either of you girls care for a refreshing drink? Your usual, Isabel?'

'No.' Isabel's face grinned teasingly up at him. Dorcas asked herself: Was it the face of a girl who had always skimmed the surface, never felt out of depth or had her emotions snarled? 'Tonight I feel . . .' The Spanish girl paused on the word . . . 'adventurous. I have the taste for something different. Surprise me,

81

Carlos.'

Dorcas very nearly missed Carlos's look of amused appreciation. Her mind was fully and unpleasantly occupied with the thought that Isabel was not as cool and unfeeling as she cared to make out.

Carlos said: 'What would you like, Dorcas?' His eyes were now on her. In them she saw a flame that beckoned and sweetly burned, a glow that met in her an answering glint of tears.

How could he look at her like this, hold her so close in spirit that they could even block Isabel out? But he could not block out the thought that although the moment was hers, the future was pledged to Isabel.

I won't ever be able to have him, she thought with a panicky, violent, self-pitying realization of truth. Everything is stacked against me. Foolish of her to hope that there was some way of controlling the twisting currents that would eventually separate them.

Memory's shutter flickered open. His mother's words came back to her. 'If Carlos played at love with Isabel, before long he would come to love her.' Her mind then reproduced Isabel's voice. Clear as a bell, she again heard Isabel say: 'Tonight I feel adventurous. Surprise me, Carlos.' If that was not an invitation to play, she did not know what was.

How long would Carlos continue to tease

the child and deny the beautiful and alluring woman she had become? And could Dorcas bear to be around to see brotherly affection quicken to a lively interest; gentleness and humour warm to desire?

She would have run from both of them that instant, but she had nowhere to run. So she remained seated, joining in the conversation, sipping from the tall frosted glass Carlos brought her, responding to the mood with as little vivacity as a robot. Until Carlos looked at her with questioning eyes and asked: 'Are you feeling unwell, Dorcas?'

She did not know how to answer his thoughtful consideration. She saw Isabel draw the discarded shawl up round her shoulders, and this gave her the inspiration to say: 'I'm cold, that's all. I haven't got as much sense as Isabel.' She managed to force a smile to her lips, but she couldn't smooth the edge from her voice as she offered the face-saving explanation: 'I didn't bring a shawl.'

Moonlight sheered the terrace with a cold, silvern touch.

'I should not have allowed you to sit out here so long,' Carlos said, instantly contrite. 'Our nights tend to be cold in contrast to the heat of the day.'

Warm, hurrying fingers grasped her arms. He used physical force to lift her to her feet. But it was an inner force that lifted and held her gaze. A strength of mind that browbeat her into submission. She had no will to look away. Then no wish to look away. He smiled. He had known this was how it would be. Her battling spirit was no match for his dominance, the superior power, the magnetism he wielded over her. His arrogance was such that he *knew*. From somewhere a thought mocked her. The woman who resists domination hasn't met her master.

His eyes laughed into hers, efficaciously, taunting her to applaud his ability to produce the result intended. Yet not in a mocking way, inviting her to share his triumph rather than scoring off her.

'Who says I want sense in my woman, eh?'

His hand on her cheek turned it to fire. He had done it again! Shattered her to a tender wreck of her normal self, then expected her to go into company looking totally unaffected.

Isabel led the way, pretending to be unaware of the tension in her wake. But her back was unnaturally stiff.

As it happened, their return to the room took second place to the arrival of another guest. The first intimation was voices, followed by a shuffle of feet, in the hall. A servant quietly entered, addressing Enrique Ruiz.

'Señor, there is a Señor West at the door.'

Enrique Ruiz's face broke into a wide grin. 'Excellent! Show him in at once.' He then explained for the benefit of the Rocas: 'Señor West is Dorcas's brother. We have been

84

expecting him. We instructed the search soon after Dorcas was hurt in that dreadful landslide while saving my Feli and little Rosita.' His thoughts lingered there for a moment. He went on, his tone more gentle, less brisk, 'He has been a difficult man to find.' Turning to Dorcas he said: 'This must be a memorable moment for you, my dear.'

Dorcas stared, pale and numb, momentarily overwhelmed. Finally she managed a wooden: 'Yes,' that emerged without the tiniest inflection of joy, causing the old señor's eyes to search hers with shrewd concern.

'Aren't you glad to be reunited with your brother?' Carlos said quietly in her ear, offering for the company at large: 'I do believe Dorcas is overcome.'

It served as a possible explanation for her apparent lack of enthusiasm. She sent him a grateful smile.

And then Michael was bursting through the door, his long stride making short work of the length of the room so that he seemed to shoot, tall and golden, in an arrow-straight line to Dorcas.

Gathering her in his arms, as though her tiniest hurt caused him untold pain, he crooned gently: 'Little sister, what have you done to yourself?'

The falseness of it stuck in her throat, prohibiting reply. But it was all right. These kind, moist-eyed, deceived people took it as another demonstration of her full heart. With perhaps one exception. She didn't think Carlos would be taken in like the rest of them.

Not that she could blame him if he was, because Michael's portrayal of a caring brother was faultless. Oh, he was clever, this brother of hers. Something—intuition?—must have told him to ignore everyone but her to the point of rudeness. His concern for her would naturally rise above the simple courtesy of first addressing the head of the house.

Remembering this omission, his hand smote across his forehead. Dorcas awarded him top marks for that touch of realism. His eyes, so like Dorcas's and yet with molten depths that made hers look pale and insignificant by comparison, turned appealingly to Enrique Ruiz. 'Señor. Please forgive me for an appalling breach of etiquette.'

Dorcas would never know how she resisted applauding, 'Bravo! Splendid performance!'

Enrique Ruiz's pointed beard jumped with approval. 'Think nothing of it. Your concern for your sister does you credit. But now I think we will give a little time to the introductions. I want you to meet my wife, my son, and our guests. Then, while a meal is being prepared for you, I will tell you all about your very brave sister to whom we are greatly indebted.'

A big tear held in Dorcas's throat, enlarging into a thought. Michael's fingerprint on any passage of her life betokened no good for her.

He would spoil everything. He always did. If there had been any hope in her that the unreality of the past few weeks could be anything more than a bitter-sweet interlude, it died a sudden death.

It had been a forlorn hope, anyway, in opposition to fact and common-sense. Perhaps there was some good in Michael's coming at that, because his presence would act as a truth serum. Had she ever truly thought that someone as remarkable in every way as Carlos would find lasting happiness with her? He had so much; she had nothing—but her innate honesty and a heart that promised to beat for him long after he'd forgotten the shape of her nose or the pitch of her laugh. She hoped he wouldn't forget too soon the girl who had entered his life by mistake, and for a short while had given it colour. She hoped she had given it colour. She hoped his memory of her lingered on the nice things . . . that it wouldn't be too terribly tarnished by anything Michael might do.

And now she came to the crux of the matter, and although she shaped the thought with extreme reluctance it was one she couldn't back away from. She was touching on the unpalatable and very real fear, the reason she hadn't wanted Michael to find her. He wouldn't be bothered that she had been very ill and that even now her leg supported her for only short distances, except in terms of how much it was worth. How much he could squeeze the Ruizs for, and he wouldn't be satisfied with a few weeks' free board and luxurious lodgings, either. He would be very subtle about it, of course. Wording it something like: 'It pains me to mention this . . . Dorcas is my sister and I must put her interests first.' He would make it sound as though he was acting on her say-so; as if the driving force was her greedy streak and he was crippled with shame to have such a mercenary sister. Only his duty as a brother made it possible for him to broach anything so delicate. Ah yes! that was the keynote. The bedrock of Michael's charm was his delicacy and taste in handling such matters. If she was *unworthy* enough to voice her disapproval he would put on a hurt face and tell her he was doing it for her. Then he would shamelessly hold out his hand for his share of the pickings. A man who couldn't wait for his own grandmother to die to get his hands on her money was capable of anything.

She wanted nothing . . . nothing. She had done what she did for Feli and Rosita spontaneously, without thought of reward. She didn't want to benefit materially. She would tell Michael so at the first opportunity. She would tell him she didn't want him here and that he must go.

Enrique Ruiz was busy with the introductions, keeping up an informative stream of chatter as he presented Michael to each person in turn. Now that Dorcas had reached a decision of sorts, she could give her attention to the scene being played before her eyes. She saw Michael as the two mothers must see him. A tall, clean-cut, pleasantly mannered young man, with charm to spare for someone, say, past the first flush of youth. Michael's winning ways delighted Señora Roca. Rose Ruiz looked smug because a compatriot of hers was showing himself up in such a good light.

And now Michael was being presented to Isabel, and it was through Isabel's eyes that Dorcas noticed the fineness and the aesthetic purity of his features. Odd, but although she had always been aware of her brother's good, even exceptional looks, she'd never quite appreciated the medieval page-boy expression, the quality of angelic innocence beneath that crown of golden hair.

It must have been there all the time, that special look. Was that why, since early childhood, she had always lost out in arguments against him? Why, into adolescence and beyond, whenever they appealed to an independent third party, the judgement was never granted in her favour? Because anybody with a face like that couldn't be capable of anything bad.

Eventually, Isabel managed to tear herself from Michael's side to come and sit by Dorcas.

Her cheeks were as pink as the fall of rose petals dusting a small round table; her mouth was soft in a smile.

'What a wonderful brother you have, Dorcas. You must be very happy to have him here with you.'

Happy to have him here? What a laugh! Dorcas was still doggedly searching her mind for a lever to get Michael out. But flatly, desperately, because even before she'd broached the subject to Michael she knew a sense of underlying hopelessness. Words would not be strong enough to expel him from the luxury of a style of living that was far removed from anything that either of them had ever before experienced.

She wanted to give the conventional reply. 'Yes, I'm happy to have Michael here.' But the lie stuck in her throat and so she hoped her smile conveyed much the same message.

Happily, Isabel seemed well satisfied. Something made Dorcas turn her head in Carlos's direction. Carlos was studying her brother. His expression was keenly assessing, but beyond that it was buttoned up and gave no clue to what opinion he had formed.

They all moved back to the dining room to be with Michael while he ate the meal that had been prepared for him. And now, through Michael, Dorcas's eyes were opened to the beauty of her surroundings. The magic of a rich man's existence.

The silver and exquisite glassware winked in the gentle glow of candles in well-spaced candelabra. After relishing the food, and the wine that came from a connoisseur's wine cellar, and pronouncing everything perfect, Michael was offered a splendid dish of fruit. Bananas curved to a pineapple shading from yellow to deep orange, in a nest of grapes, nectarines and peaches. Michael made his inspection and asked for a slice of the pineapple which he said looked absolutely delicious. Having no initial shyness to overcome and being of an adaptable disposition, her brother was lapping it all up.

CHAPTER FIVE

There wasn't a moment to lose. If she was to get Michael out she must act quickly, before he grew too accustomed to the elegance and perfection within these lovely walls.

Before going to her room she made a point of asking one of the maids which room Michael had been given. She didn't undress. She sat out on the balcony. The air was cooling on her cheeks. Flower beds and shrubbery alike took on monstrous, leaping shapes in the moonlight. Lights from the villa plunged into the shadowy recesses of the night. She sat, not in peace and tranquillity, but in agitation, nerving herself for the ordeal facing her.

She waited until every light in the villa had been turned out, and still she didn't move, but allowed what she considered to be sufficient time for everybody to have got off to sleep. Michael also, very probably. If so, she would just have to wake him up for the confrontation. Perhaps it would have been kinder in that respect to wait until morning, but that would be just another example of putting off. It now seemed silly and melodramatic to have waited until everybody was asleep. Although it would have been a natural thing to do, she hadn't wanted the fuss of accompanying her brother to his room when he retired. This way had seemed better, although now she suspected she had been giving way to delaying tactics. If she waited until morning, her resolution would have faltered still further.

She stole along the gallery, her heels making the faintest whisper as she moved past closed doors. As she stopped at the right door she took a deep breath before closing her fingers round the knob. She hoped Michael hadn't locked his door. She didn't want to knock and run the risk of attracting unwanted attention. It yielded and she was inside.

Her brother had left the shutters open and so the room wasn't in total darkness. Cautiously negotiating the pieces of furniture, she crossed to the bed. Her fingers stroked its flatness and her forehead was just beginning to pleat at the puzzle of it when a voice, male, but definitely not Michael's voice, said from the depth of an armchair: 'Would you mind telling me what you are doing in my room?'

Dorcas spun round to face—of all people—Carlos. Her mouth flew open in shock; she couldn't speak until she'd swallowed rapidly for several seconds. Even then all she managed was a croak.

'Would you believe looking for my brother?'

She looked small and innocent and no one could have disbelieved.

Carlos chose to raise a doubting eyebrow. 'Really! Do you think I've got him hidden in the wardrobe?'

'Don't be ridiculous!' She bit hard on the inside of her cheek. 'It's perfectly obvious I've mistaken the room. I am looking for my brother.'

'And if he catches you here, he'll be looking for me. Pistols at dawn.'

Her chin lifted. She could feel her cheeks growing blotchy, and sighed on the relief that it was too dark for him to see this.

He conceded: 'I suppose anyone who can wander into the wrong garden can also blunder into the wrong bedroom.'

The gentle quality of his teasing relaxed her. 'I'm glad it's your bedroom.'

'Are you?' He sounded amused.

'Yes.' Her nod was emphatic. 'I don't have to explain to you what I wanted to see Michael about.'

'A pity. I rather hoped you would. It must be something pretty important that it won't keep until morning.'

'I thought it was.'

'But not any more?'

'I can't tell you.' Her fingers twisted nervously. 'Please don't probe because at this hour one is usually at a low ebb. I might just be tempted to tell. And you are the last person I should confide in.'

'Oh?' His tone was faintly piqued.

'You sound . . . funny. You're not cross with me, are you?'

'Of course not! It's your privilege to choose whether to confide or not,' he said crossly. Then he laughed. 'M'm, yes. I see what you mean. But look, it's my low ebb hour too, and my temptations are every bit as great as yours even though they do follow a different course. I think you'd better go back to your room.'

'I suppose I'd better,' she said.

She didn't feel in a compromising situation. She felt so safe. She looked up at him with her heart in her eyes, willing him not to send her away. She had never been in love before. She didn't know what to do with it; she didn't know whether to ignore it, or own to it.

If she were honest with herself, she wanted to own to it; she wanted to tell him, as simply as she could, how she felt. But she didn't. She knew it would be silly to let words of love come between them. The love was only on her side. His feelings towards her were physical. By owning her love she would close a door between them. Under that arrogant exterior was a man of deep and honourable convictions. If he was aware of the tender condition of her heart, in future he would refrain from teasing her and sparring with her. Half a loaf was better than none.

Sighing, she bid him a reluctant goodnight, and turned to go to her room.

It wasn't until she was in bed, her knees drawn up to her chin in her favourite thinking position, that it occurred to her that he had been fully dressed. She wondered what problem had kept him out of his bed.

Dorcas resolved not to be put off, but to tackle Michael first thing in the morning. Now, more than ever, he must not be allowed to indulge his eye for an easy pick-up. She meant money, but it came to her that the household was rich in pretty maids. Besides her own Teresa, there were girls who cleaned the rooms and served at the table. Although they seemed happy in their work, because of the isolation of the villa they must feel a bit cut off from life. She didn't want Michael to turn a head, and leave a broken heart.

For all her good intentions, that day didn't offer one single moment for the confrontation she dreaded more and more as the minutes ticked off. In deploring the predicament she was in, she didn't regret the circumstances that had led up to it. Given her time again, she wouldn't alter a thing. And yet, a lingering part of her mind strayed back to her happy-go-lucky outlook in the carefree days before Carlos entered her life.

Next day the opportunity she looked for presented itself. She spotted Michael in a quiet corner of the terrace keeping company with nothing more off-putting than a large drink. Yet off-put she was. She walked towards him with a sinking heart.

He observed her from a distance and, as always when she was conscious of being watched, her limp—which some days passed unnoticed—was more pronounced.

'Dorcas the Porkas,' he said. 'I used to call you that when you were a porky infant. Do you remember?'

She pulled forward a chair and sat down. 'I remember.' And hated it, she thought.

'And now you're nothing but skin and bones. And you've got a poorly leg as well. Poor pet. Does it hurt?'

'No.' It didn't—well, not much. And anyway she wouldn't tell him if it did. Except that physical pain might explain the shadows in her eyes. And under them.

Unexpectedly, Michael reached out and touched the smudged crescents. 'You don't look too cracky to me. This business has knocked you out more than you think.' Although his glance was not unkindly, it incorporated a shrewd and cunning look that Dorcas shrank back from. Long experience of the workings of her brother's mind clued her what to expect next. Neither did she trust his deceptively soft and friendly mood. 'I had a long talk with Papa Ruiz yesterday. The old boy thinks highly of you.' Even the expected can be shattering, and Dorcas heard out Michael's verdict with sinking dread. 'If you play your cards right you could be on a good thing.'

'What a horrible idea!' she said, letting her outrage rip. 'I don't want to be on a good thing. I feel guilty enough as it is, being kept and not doing a hand's stir in return.'

Her battling reaction came up against a wall of teasing indulgence that Michael erected without effort.

Benignly he said: 'Never thought to see the day my sister would admit to being a kept woman. Hey!' As Dorcas tensed—'That was supposed to be a joke. You're not well enough to work.'

'Don't you think I know that,' she snapped back, burning on Michael's envious cool. 'What do you think keeps me here?'

'That's my sister! Seeing how the other half lives, that's what! Only you would want to leave it.'

'I don't like the idea of being dependent on strangers,' she said stubbornly.

He groaned softly. 'You're a bigger nutter than I thought. Listen to me, girl. They're going to pay for what happened to you. And I'm just the boy to see they pay good.'

'That's my brother! Just about the most mercenary man I know.' She was really angry now; angry and frustrated—it was impossible to get through to him. It was like hitting a brick wall with a feather. 'This is what I'm afraid of. I forbid you to make any mention of a reward.'

His eyes narrowed to amused slits. 'You forbid?' He was perfectly at ease, completely unruffled. 'On the level, Dor, you're too independent. That's always been your trouble. You need someone to look after you.'

'You?' she suggested, swallowing on mock sweetness.

'What's so surprising about that? I don't like to see you down.'

'I've been down before, Michael. I don't remember your bothering about me then.'

She'd needed him then, just after their grandmother died. How she had needed an affectionate older brother to lean on. But Michael had made it abundantly clear that he didn't want the appendage of a grief-stricken kid sister.

Her shaft went home. 'Point taken,' he said, looking uncomfortable. 'Kick me if you want to. You can't kick me any harder than I've kicked myself. I'm not going to run away from the issue, or pretend it never happened, because it did happen—I left you when you most needed me—and all the pretending in the world can't wipe it out. I acted like a louse. The thing I ask myself is why did I act like this? Because I was spoilt rotten, or was that my reaction to grief? You tell me because I don't know. I'll probably never know. But I'll tell you this, I'm not going to bury it away in my mind and forget about it. Not until I've learnt from it first.'

Michael thinking deep—regretting. She didn't believe it. *Did* she believe it?

She said tentatively, without condemnation:

99

'Everybody does something stupid at some time or other. One's mistakes and stupidities are supposed to be the stepping stones one climbs to better things.'

Was that what he was saying? Was he hoodwinking her? His apparent sincerity overwhelmed her and she felt pin-pricks of hope attacking her scalp. But she'd known the cynical, unfeeling Michael too long to accept unconditionally this made-to-specification new model brother.

'What gives, Michael? Really?'

'If you must know, I'm more than a bit shattered about you. If only I'd bundled you off to France with me.'

She had a sudden crazy urge to giggle. 'Now I'm sure you don't mean that. What would you want with a sister with all those French birds,' she said with a flash of cruel candidness, using his vernacular.

'Straight up! I was worried about you. *Am* worried about you,' he repeated insistently.

His eyes were frank and unsmiling; she was no match for the gush of emotion that swamped her.

She blew her nose and dabbed at her eyes and gulped. And perhaps she was a gullible fool at that, but it was a special sort of joy to hear him say: 'And you're not going to tell me to go away. That would increase the agony now that I've seen how ill you look. It would be criminal of you to ask it of me. If I couldn't see you every day I should start wondering if you were making satisfactory progress, or getting worse, and kicking myself afresh for going off and leaving you.'

Dorcas had never professed to be a hard-hearted girl and he did look caring. In the event she lulled her qualms and pointed out: 'It's not up to me to say whether you go or stay.'

'Señor Ruiz asked me to stay for as long as it pleased me.'

He slanted Dorcas a guarded look and risked: 'But if my presence makes you feel uneasy, you've only to say the word and I'll pack up and go. I feel as though I've done enough damage already.'

Dorcas touched his hand. 'You haven't done anything. Nobody can accept that sort of responsibility. Stay.'

'Do you want me to?'

She swallowed. 'Yes, I do. Michael?'

'M'm?'

'Were you having a good time in France?'

'M'm.'

'You seem different, somehow.'

'In what way?'

'Nicer. Did you meet anyone on your travels?' She wondered if a special girl was behind his nicer disposition.

'I met lots of people.'

'I mean someone special.'

'There was Sam.'

'All right, I get the message. If you did meet a special girl, you're not telling.' A mischievous smile sat on her lips. 'I hope being dragged here didn't spoil anything for you.'

*   *   *

Feli, her husband Jaime, and adorable little Rosita arrived for a weekend visit. The exuberance of Feli's greeting brought the tears stinging to Dorcas's eyes.

Clasping her arms about her shoulders and kissing her warmly on the cheek, Feli said: 'This show of affection is permitted. What we have been through makes us . . . almost sisters.' She looked at Dorcas, shook her head at what she saw, and said amusingly: 'My almost sister is too thin and pale. Come to my house and I will feed you paella and trout baked with ham in wine, and steak served with stuffed aubergines. And masses of cream-filled pastries. And then,' she said laughingly putting her hands to her own small waist, 'you will be plump like me. What do you say, Jaime?'

Jaime had a long thin face, interesting looking rather than handsome, with kind eyes beneath thickly defined eyebrows. A moustache followed the line of his laughing upper lip.

'I think at times you are plump in the head.' To Dorcas he said: 'I second my wife's invitation. The door of our house will always

102

be open to you.' He didn't say 'For what you did for Feli and Rosita,' but it was there in his eyes.

Without words a friendship was established. She knew that whatever happened she could always rely on the support of Feli's husband.

She had made some good friends. Rose Ruiz, who was genuine in her affection for her, even though she lived in daily dread that her son might also feel affection for Dorcas. Her kindly señor. Dorcas knew she could count on Enrique Ruiz's friendship for life. Feli. Even Carlos's tart-tongued grandmother had warmed to her. And now Jaime. It seemed unjust that if she did have to fade quietly out of Carlos's life, she would have to move herself out of the orbit of his family. Not only would she have to give him up, but she would also have to surrender these good friendships.

Her eyes felt moist—was it weakness that kept sending her in an emotional spin?—and she was glad to bury her face in Rosita's neck and kiss and fuss the little girl with the melting smile.

The seconds whirled off the clock that weekend. With just three extra people, the house seemed to have filled with laughter and light and, as a bonus, Rosita took her first tottering steps. One, two, three and then—smack—down she'd go on her well-padded bottom. Then she would hold her hands out to be picked up by Dor-dor, which was the best she could make of Dorcas's name.

Life was all roses. Even Rose Ruiz, distracted by the presence of her granddaughter, was less watchful of Dorcas. Michael was behaving in an exemplary manner. He made a point of seeking her out to slip an arm round her with brotherly predilection. He would nuzzle her neck and his grin incorporated the smiles of a million angels. 'How goes it, kid? Forgiven me for trying to tilt your pretty ideals?'

This was an old argument. She knew he thought she let sentimentality distort her perspective. Big of him to give in, to allow her her pretty ideals as he called this stubbornness of hers in not wanting to extract financial reward from the Ruizs. Poor Michael, he still considered pride to be cold comfort in comparison with the things money could buy.

Which made his present attitude all the more marvellous. Unless? Well, she hated herself for nourishing the tiniest seed of distrust, but could he be pretending to let her have her own way because he was wise enough to know that an opposed ideal is apt to gain in strength?

The weekend was so much fun that even that thought wasn't sufficiently discouraging to wipe out the sparkle for her.

Carlos remarked at the change in her. 'You are looking much better.' He took her face between his hands, scrutinizing it fiercely.

'Perhaps you should accept Feli's invitation to go and stay with her. My clever sister seems to have acquired the trick of putting a smile on your lips.'

Quite suddenly the smile had to be fixed there, because it was in danger of slithering down into a frown. Did Carlos mean that he wanted her out of the house? Had she over-stayed her welcome? Ought she to take Feli up on her invitation and leave with them when they went tomorrow?

'I have to go away soon,' Carlos told her. 'There is a business trip I must make. One which I have been putting off.'

Feelings, the impossible love she felt for Carlos, swamped her. As her inside churned she knew clearly that her idea of accompanying Feli and her family in the morning was a passing thought she had no intention of following up. She couldn't tear herself away from Carlos, not while the thought of his going away erupted like a protest . . . a protesting and painful shock in her brain, a desolate coldness in her stomach.

She felt angry. She hadn't asked for this. Completely against her will her life had changed course. Who had given the permission for these drastic changes? She hadn't. It had promised so much . . . was the promise to be broken? It wasn't as if she'd ever thirsted for adventure. In her dull, plodding way she had been content with her drab

105

existence. Only it hadn't seemed drab then. She'd had nothing to compare it with. She didn't know that life could contain such colour that her other life—already so remote that it seemed to have been lived by another girl, in another age almost—was no more than a flickering grey image of escaping memories. After knowing all this, how could she go back to *that*?

Her mind stood quietly on that thought for a few seconds. Then reason returned. She had never rated more than a slim chance of holding Carlos. This was the thought she must freeze on her mind. She couldn't imagine spending the rest of her life without Carlos . . . the rest of her life trailed out, an awfully long time . . . but she might have to.

*   *   *

The Rocas came to dinner for Feli's last evening. Isabel wore a dress of deep apricot shading to a bodice of palest peach. Against her exotic colouring it looked wonderful. Dorcas could hardly take her eyes off her.

When Jaime said of her own cornflower blue: 'Very becoming,' she took it that he was being kind because he was her friend.

That evening there was much gaiety and just a hint of sadness. In the morning Feli and her family were going home and they would be sadly missed. It added the touch of poignancy to the party spirit.

Dorcas found herself being drawn into conversation by don Alfonso, Isabel's papa, and discovered him to be a sensitive and intelligent man. Michael divided himself equally between Isabel and her mama, entertaining them with his quick, witty brain. His clowning made doña Maria laugh until the tears ran down her plump face. Isabel's cheeks were pink with delight.

Observing them, don Alfonso remarked: 'Your brother is a very talented young man.'

'Talented, señor?' Dorcas queried. Michael was playing the fool. Delightfully so. But was that a talent?

'See how easily he eclipses every man present. Without effort he has my wife and daughter sitting in the palm of his hand. Any firm would welcome that sort of flair in an employee. Does your brother speak Spanish or Portuguese?'

'A little of both. Only enough to get by, though.'

'No matter. That young man would soon become fluent.'

'What are you thinking, señor?' Dorcas eased forward, trying to probe beyond the speculative gleam in don Alfonso's eye.

'I'm thinking several things. Lacking your brother's very special charm, I'm thinking that I'm glad I have reached an age when it is no longer the first importance to compete for the

107

attention of the womenfolk. I am thinking that this sort of charm plays a vital part in any sales drive, and that your brother would be capable of squeezing a large wine order from a staunch abstainer. I am thinking that any time he wants to change his employment, I hope he will approach me because he will be an asset to any sales organization.'

'Do you want me to mention this to my brother, señor?' said Dorcas, frowning slightly. Her biggest hope was that Michael would quickly tire of the quietness of the district. She did not want to be even slightly instrumental in keeping him here.

Don Alfonso moved his thumb thoughtfully across his chin. His observant eyes were pinned on his daughter's animated face.

'Let us not be too hasty,' he decided. 'Don't mention anything just yet, There is an aspect of the situation that requires some further thought.'

Dorcas wondered what aspect he referred to, but only fleetingly because Carlos was towering above them enquiring: 'Is this a select twosome or may I be permitted to join?'

'How is it,' complained don Alfonso with a buccaneerish twinkle, 'that when I am making progress with a beautiful señorita, along comes a dashing *caballero* to cut me out?' He stood up, robustly slapping Carlos on the back. 'Have my seat. It is time I had a word with your esteemed father.'

Before he walked away his finger went up across his lips, reminding Dorcas to keep quiet about their conversation. He had no idea how happy she was to oblige.

Carlos sat down, stuck out his legs in the inelegant way men do, and smiled intimately into her eyes. 'Hello there,' he said.

Irrationally, stupidly and irrevocably the tender moment was lost to her because she didn't know how to hold it. Who but Dorcas would draw attention to the popularity of one man to another; who but Dorcas would turn the conversation in just this way?

'Michael seems to be making a hit with the ladies.'

That look of boyish softness ebbed from Carlos's features leaving his face cardboard stiff. 'So it would appear.'

Rose Ruiz and Feli had now joined Isabel and her mama and all four were hinged on Michael's every word. Carlos resentful of Michael's moment of social triumph? Carlos jealous? Could be. Bringing to mind what don Alfonso had said, Dorcas realized that Carlos was of an age to compete. And yet, looking at Carlos, Dorcas wouldn't have said he envied her brother's gregarious personality, but that he saw through it. She thought it would be nearer the mark to say that Carlos was a shrewder judge of character than the others.

*   *   *

Next day, Feli, Jaime and Rosita left for home, after extracting a promise from Dorcas that she would not leave Spain without visiting them. The wording shocked her senses. Did they know she was mentally packing her suitcase, that she needed but the slightest push to send her on her way?

*   *   *

A house is all the quieter for having known a child. How sorely the *pequeña* was missed. Dorcas had not realized how fully Rosita had occupied both her hands and her thoughts until she went, leaving her mind free to worry about Michael again.

He went out most evenings and although Dorcas tossed out delicate enquiries, Michael maintained a mysterious silence about his activities. Although she fretted over this, she was not her brother's keeper and she was powerless to do anything. She only hoped that whoever was responsible for the gleam in her brother's eye was mature enough to know that Michael was a lot of a knave in his dealings with women. Thrilled and flattered the girl of the moment might be, but she could get ready to blow on her fingers. And consider herself lucky if she escaped with only a mild scorching!

One blessing, it seemed to have got through

to Michael that she wanted nothing from the Ruizs beyond the hospitality they were so generously extending. All was blissfully silent on that subject.

One evening as they were all seated round the table—yet another occasion when the Rocas were dinner guests—don Enrique brought a special bottle of wine up from the cellar.

'Today is by way of being a celebration,' he said.

Dorcas's unguarded eye flew from Isabel to Carlos. For an agonized moment she thought that Carlos might have spoken for Isabel and she wondered how she could possibly raise her glass to their future happiness.

The sparkling liquid was poured into crystal glasses with air and colour twist stems. Dorcas lifted hers, marvelling that she could act normally when the meaning was about to be snuffed from her life; when she was breaking up inside because her tenderest and most passionate feelings had been given to a man who had no use for them. She swallowed, and composed herself for the señor's announcement.

Surprisingly, his kindly eyes rested on her. 'Dorcas has dispensed with the services of the physiotherapist who has been attending her. Perhaps as an old man I shouldn't notice such things, but today also, Dorcas discarded her long skirts and I have been happy to observe that her skin is not as terribly scarred as she once feared it might be. Isn't that worth drinking to?'

Giving Dorcas a boisterous wink, Michael said: 'From the way she's been hiding her legs, you wouldn't think they'd stop a fella's eyes as dead as a duck full of buckshot.'

Dorcas gasped. It was a remark better fitted to a bawdry pub atmosphere than a genteel home setting.

'A fella?' puzzled Isabel. 'A man, *sí*? But stop his eyes as dead as what did you say? This I do not understand.'

'What it means,' Carlos explained with a remarkably straight face, 'is that Dorcas has got nice legs.'

Dorcas blushed. Relief mingled with her laughter. She was still wallowing in the rich feeling of reprieve because the señor had not announced his son's engagement to Isabel, when Michael swayed to his feet.

His eyes were as bright as those of a child's who is sitting on a tight secret. His mood was devil-may-care. Ebullient. With a sinking heart Dorcas realized he'd had more to drink than was good for him.

Lifting his glass with a flourish that was almost theatrical, he toasted: 'My sister! The unappreciated light of my life. She may not have the brilliance of the sun, but she has the constancy of the moon. If ill-fortune had not struck, this quality would have carried her to the stardom she so coveted.'

Dorcas flung to her feet. 'My brother has had too much to drink,' she claimed. 'He doesn't know what he's saying.'

She tried to damp down her anger and frustration, but it was too late. Don Enrique was looking at her through puzzled eyes. Later he would sift. His immediate concern was to make his guests feel at ease and soothe the English girl his family owed so much to—perhaps more than he realized. He loved this child and could so easily slot her into the place of a second daughter.

'You must not distress yourself,' he instructed Dorcas, reaching across the table to pat her hand.

Michael sat down, flushed, smiling, sending his sister a look of sharp mischief that heightened the colour in her cheeks.

This time the new protest forming in her throat was stemmed by Carlos's disconcerting gaze. She *knew* she had protested too much already. If she'd kept quiet, Michael's treachery might have been taken for drunken ramblings. Her vehemence had given his words meaning.

'If you will excuse me, please, I would like to go to my room.' She spoke now with about as much force as a spent match.

It was Carlos who assisted her to the door, opened it for her and followed her out. His hand claimed her elbow and he steered her away from the stairs leading to the sanctuary of her room, and drew her towards the terrace.

The night air was cool, but his voice was warm and understanding.

'It's all right. I'm not going to question you. I know.'

As Dorcas digested this, the only sound was a metallic rustling of leaves. It was a monochromatic setting. Light from the villa made patterns on the floor. Carlos's dinner jacket merged with the night. The shadows that stole the green from her dress and coloured it moonlight, etched his features in black and ivory relief.

The smile he gave her, so sweetly comforting and kindly intentioned, in peaceful harmony with the surroundings, was the one perfected by man down the centuries. Dorcas was too starched with pride to smile back.

'What do you know?' she said stiffly, wishing she could let his gentleness and caring influence the mood, yet not being able to find one spark of response in her entire system.

'I know that you were a dancer. That the injury to your leg finished your career.'

'Michael was wrong. I couldn't have got to the top.'

'Modestly and predictably answered.'

'No. Honestly answered. I quit while I was in front. Just now when you said you knew, you did mean you knew before this evening?'

He seemed reluctant to answer that. A

secret glimmered in his eye. Contemplation chose not to shadow it with a lie. 'Yes. I've known quite a while.'

'Michael had already told you? That exhibition just now was for nothing!'

'Michael didn't tell me.'

'No? Then who did?'

'Don't you know?'

The concern in his eyes brought the tears rushing to hers. She gritted her teeth and said: 'If I knew I wouldn't be asking.'

'You told me yourself.'

'Why don't I remember telling you?'

'It was while you were in hospital.'

'Ah . . . yes!'

'Why do you say "Ah . . . yes!' in just that way?'

'Because it has bothered me a lot. I've kept feeling there was something I should remember, but couldn't. There's a lot about my first week in hospital that I don't remember.'

'What do you remember?'

'The nearness of you. Nothing concrete. Impressions of things. Nice things. You held my hand. There were just the two of us in this small, shadowy world and . . .'

'Go on.'

'I can't. That's what always happens. The memory starts to come, but never does, and I'm left tantalizingly in the air.'

'You said nothing to bring a blush to your

cheeks.'

'May I be the judge of that?'

'Your main concern was that we shouldn't feel guilty or indebted to you. After making sure that Feli and Rosita were all right, that was your first thought. It didn't seem to occur to you to ask if you were going to be all right. Your only thought of self was a certain preoccupation with the loss of a pair of ballet shoes. You were—are—so terribly prickly. So afraid that we might dare to want to reward you. Shame on you, Dorcas West! Did you really think we could use you and then cast you carelessly to one side?'

With heightening anxiety, Dorcas searched his gaze. Had she made a terrible mistake in thinking he was attracted to her? In his eyes did she see, flitting across the tender teasing, gratitude and pity? The two emotions she wanted none of!

Her thoughts made her angry. Her anger was directed against herself. Why couldn't she take it at face value? Why this insatiable need to probe? Carlos was right. She was prickly. And prone to suspicion. The voices in her head shouted louder than the voice in her heart which was telling her that no one who was only pretending affection could be so convincing. The very real danger was, if she didn't listen to that solitary small voice, if she continued to be suspicious of his every word and on guard when he demonstrated affection,

116

she could well be throwing away something that was dear and precious for something that didn't exist.

'I never said a proper thank you for your kindness to me while I was in hospital.' Her voice was husky.

He said, 'I got more out of it than I gave.' Yet his lips did not move. His eyes said it for him.

How could anyone with her training—she had been taught expression through movement in Ballet School—doubt his sincerity? Ballet is a story told without words. 'I love you', 'I hate you', 'Come', 'Go', can be expressed with a flexed hand, the eyes, the stiffness or suppleness of the body.

Yet if Dorcas had never had a ballet lesson in her life, she would have understood the message his eyes were conveying.

'Dorcas. A few days ago I told you I had to go away on a business trip. It has been brought forward. I have to go tomorrow. My reaction on being told was that I did not want to leave you at this particular moment. I thought the timing was bad. Now I think perhaps the timing is not so bad. My absence will give you time to reflect. When I return I am going to ask you a question. You know what that question is. Think about it while I am away. Have your answer prepared for when I return.'

CHAPTER SIX

Usually, Dorcas had no difficulty in getting her hair to go the way she wanted it. But this morning, when she particularly wanted to be early for breakfast, it refused to be combed into submission and took ten frustrating minutes before it went right. By the time she ventured downstairs, she had an idea that Carlos would have left on his business trip.

Certainly there was no sign of him as Rose Ruiz greeted her from the breakfast table. 'Good morning, Dorcas. Did you sleep well?'

'Good morning, señora. I should say I slept too well, judging by the clock.'

'But that is good. Perhaps something has happened to make you feel more relaxed. I have my own theory on how to guarantee sound sleep.'

'And what is that, señora?' Dorcas dutifully asked.

'A clear conscience, child. Doing what I know in my heart is right, even though, as is often the case, it is not always the thing my heart would wish.'

'Life can be exceedingly difficult,' Dorcas said, sighing in full agreement.

'I think that is part of the pattern. Life is a testing ground. It sets up a series of problems and it is how we acquit ourselves that writes the final report.'

Blade-slim in her denim-blue sundress, Dorcas protectively clutched her midriff. She saw the breakfast setting, the white tablecloth, the coffee pot now being lifted in Rose Ruiz's capable hand; the dainty cup, appropriately patterned with a rose border, being handed to her. Another movement alerted her senses and drew her gaze beyond the sphere of breakfast rolls and preserves, to the sun-warmed stones of the terrace wall richly draped in its carelessly flung shawl of bougainvillaea. Or, more specifically, to the man standing there.

Aware of being under the microscope of Rose Ruiz's scrutiny, Dorcas modified her smile. 'Hello, Carlos,' she told the approaching figure.

Rose Ruiz's chin swung round in surprise. 'Carlos! What are you still doing here? I thought you'd gone.'

'Without saying goodbye to you, Mother,' he reproved, a trifle disingenuously Dorcas thought.

Neither was Rose Ruiz taken in. 'I should have known,' she said drily. Then with warmth: 'Goodbye, Carlos. Take care.'

Straightening up from kissing his mother's delicately flushed cheek, Carlos revealed the true reason for his delayed departure. 'Walk with me to the car, Dorcas. I want to talk to you.'

Dorcas got to her feet. The texture of her

119

composure wasn't as smooth as she would have wished as she accompanied Carlos down the terrace steps.

Barely were they out of earshot when he said: 'I should have left an hour ago, but I deliberately waited to see you. I thought you were never going to wake up.'

'You should have sent someone to rouse me.'

'I have the patience to wait.' His smile, starting in his eyes and spreading warmly to his lips, gave the words a deeper, more exciting meaning.

'You look surprised?'—as Dorcas made a small, involuntary gasp. 'Would you not have accredited me with the characteristic of having patience?'

'You know it's not that at all.'

'Only you would put me in my place quite so bluntly. Of course, I confess that you are right. I do know.' His voice changed subtly. 'I like to tease you.'

Having arrived at his car, which he had previously driven out of the garage and parked in the driveway in readiness for his departure, Dorcas attempted to blow common sense on her thoughts. 'You haven't told me why you wanted to see me.'

'Ah . . . yes! There is something I want to ask you. I want you to do something for me.' Reading the startled expression in her eyes he said, not unkindly: 'This is in no way related to

120

the question I referred to last night. That must wait until I return.'

'Then ask away,' she invited, swallowing on conflicting emotions of disappointment and relief that it was something else, say of a less disturbing nature. Some basic spark in her enjoyed being verbally seduced by him.

Unexpectedly, he said: 'I want you to keep an eye on my father. Two years ago he had a slight warning of what might happen if he didn't ease up.'

'What kind of warning? Do you mean—his heart?' Dorcas asked, with hers in her eyes. In the short time she had known him, she had become very fond of Enrique Ruiz. It troubled her to think that her kind señor was not in the best of health.

'Yes. He has been reasonably good. He takes gentle, regular exercise as prescribed, and no longer puts in excessive hours at his desk. But worry and stress are not so easily dealt with. My reason for going on this business trip is to bring about a situation of less worry for my father. He assures me he has absolute trust in my judgement, but I think he has yet to convince himself that I know what I am doing. While I am away he is going to brood on the matter. Old dogs do not easily hand over the reins to young pups. In my absence I am deputizing you to keep an especially watchful eye on him. Don't let him dwell on business matters. Distract him with some of that inconsequential chatter you women are reputably famous for.'

'Oh, I will,' said Dorcas, not taking exception to that disparaging remark about women. For one thing they do chatter, and for another there isn't a female born who doesn't feel uplifted to be doing something to help the man she loves. 'I will,' she repeated, carried away by her own enthusiasm, both fascinated and repelled by the bold, pushing question poised on her tongue. 'Will it mean the merger with Señor Roca is not of top priority?'

'No. For the survival of both firms, that must come about.' His brows drew into a formidable line. 'Who told you of this merger? Not my father?'

'No. Your mother told me,' said Dorcas bleakly, despising herself for tale-bearing, but too deep in to do otherwise.

'Did she!'—thoughtfully. 'And what else did my mother say?'—perceptively. 'You might as well tell me. Your face already has.'—persistently.

Regretting her give-away expression, Dorcas showed spirit as she formed the self-destructive words. 'Why don't you marry Isabel Roca? That, surely, would be the sensible way out of the dilemma.'

He reached out, drawing a cool finger down her hot cheek. His eyes captured the emotions tightly embracing her features.

'This is the face I will carry in my mind. In

122

return, I will leave you with this thought. I have sufficient sense to distrust the easy solution.'

Dorcas had two distinct impressions. One, that she had crossed a raging fiord, leaving safe ground for terrain unknown. That having crossed she could not go back. The second impression was to do with Carlos. He was displeased with her for thinking his integrity would permit him to seek the easy solution.

He confounded her by saying: 'I am not angry with you. Disappointed, perhaps, that you do not know me better.'

And then she was once again gathered into the orbit of his smile as his fingers outlined her mouth in a gesture that both remonstrated and forgave, and was more moving than a kiss.

'Despite the fact that you rose late this morning, I think you did not sleep well last night.'

'No. I had . . . things on my mind.'

'Not something to do with the question I am going to ask you on my return?'

'Not something, Carlos. Everything. The importance you have given it makes it obvious what the question is. It is that one, isn't it?'

Her eagerness tempted a smile to his lips. 'Yes, it is that one,' he said in a gentle voice.

'But you of all people must know that it's not possible.'

'Dorcas, I cannot tell you how heartening I find your words. I can't tell you now, I mean, because there isn't time. But when I come back . . .' His voice was full of regret at parting. 'I must go, *querida.*'

Querida! He had called her darling.

His fingers briefly touched her cheek. He got in his car and drove off.

She watched him go, feeling troubled and happy. Of the two emotions, happiness was uppermost. *He had called her darling.* And when he came back he was . . . what else could the question be but a proposal of marriage? *He was going to ask her to marry him.*

The thought, 'It is not possible,' turned round and became, 'Perhaps Carlos can make it possible.' Please, please let his invincible will make it possible. And please, please let him be motivated by love, and not pity and gratitude.

She would have to tell Michael off for airing his surmise that her act of heroism had cost her her dancing career. But it was not a matter of extreme urgency any more because she had previously divulged this information to Carlos during her period of insensibility in hospital. When eventually she did speak to her brother, her words would be tempered by the thought that Michael sincerely believed it was the injury to her leg and not her lack of star quality that would curtail her ambitions. It is difficult to sustain anger towards someone who battles under the flag of sincerity. Dorcas was half ready to believe her brother had spoken what he thought to be the truth. And if further explanation was required for her mood of benign forgiveness, who could be unforgiving and angry while bubbling—dazed and dizzy—with happiness? Not Dorcas.

The day that would be lightened with thoughts of Carlos, if not his presence, stretched before her. How to fill her time was becoming an increasing problem. In a normal home she would have helped her hostess with the domestic chores. It would never become common or garden for Dorcas to have her room tidied and cleaned for her and eat a meal that wasn't paid for in physical effort. When she lived with her grandmother, she had been responsible for buying in the provisions and cooking the meals. She liked cooking, experimenting with new recipes and perfecting old ones. And later, suffering a series of landladies' indifferent cooking, she had conscientiously helped with the clearing away and washing up.

She decided to broach the subject of her inactivity with her hostess. Rose Ruiz was sitting where they had left her. She looked up from the note-pad on which she was jotting notes on what seemed to be a menu.

'Isn't it a beautiful morning? Not too hot, with a touch of breeze. Carlos should have a pleasant journey. He is a good son. I am a very lucky woman.'

'My grandmother had her own theory about that. On hearing an envious remark about somebody's luck in having something, a possession or a perfect friendship, she had ready this stock reply. Yes, they are lucky. And the harder they work, the luckier they become.'

Rose Ruiz laughed in spontaneous delight. 'Your grandmother was a very wise woman. It's true that I've worked hard at my luck. A perfect marriage, a happy home atmosphere, inner content, do not just happen. These things must be helped. It is difficult at the best of times, without starting off with a handicap.'

'And it would be a severe handicap if Carlos passed over Isabel Roca for me. I think,' said Dorcas, her mouth going wry, 'it would be a miracle.'

'I would not go as far as to say that,' was the thoughtful reply. 'A little unexpected, perhaps.' Rose Ruiz maintained her smile as her mind took a long step back in time. 'The handicap I referred to was not a future possibility in the event, likely or otherwise, of an alliance between you and my son, but to . . .' Snapping the confidence off there, leaving it for Dorcas to ponder over later, she said tantalizingly: 'You have a quality that is very rare. You are a good listener. As a rule, young girls are too full of their own importance to make good listeners. Not only are you that, but you listen in such a way as to invite the indiscretion that is later regretted. I will be on guard in future, Dorcas. You will not draw me so easily again.'

126

Dorcas said, just a little hurt: 'You compliment me if you think I deliberately schemed to make you say something better retained.'

'I compliment you, Dorcas, but not on that score. There is not an atom of guile in you. You are the sweetest girl I have ever met, which makes it . . .' Her tongue made a clicking sound. 'Tch! And for all my protestations to the contrary, I almost did it again. Talked too much.' She glanced into Dorcas's thoughtful face and smiled. 'Now, tell me what you are going to do today.'

Dorcas sighed. 'Nothing, señora. The same as I did yesterday and the day before that too. That is what I came to talk to you about. Is there something, a household chore perhaps, that I could do?'

'My dear, I already have the unenviable task of soothing Teresa who complains daily about this inconsiderate girl who makes her own bed and tidies her clothes away.'

The faintest smile warmed round Dorcas's lips. 'Teresa won't have need to complain about me today. I was in too much of a hurry to come to breakfast to make my bed, and I seem to remember abandoning things, my nightgown and my shower cap, as I went. But seriously, surely there is something I can do?'

'We both know, Dorcas, that my husband would not permit you to do a proper job of work, but if I think of anything . . .'

'Anything at all,' Dorcas eagerly interrupted, knowing her hostess was speaking to pacify.

'. . . I promise to let you know.'

Although Dorcas had taken short walks, she had not yet tested her leg on a long walk. On the principle of no time like the present, Dorcas offered the thought for Rose Ruiz's approval.

'Yes, a walk will do you good. I would volunteer to accompany you if it didn't sound so energetic. And if it wasn't my day to have the members of my sewing circle to lunch. I'm being very naughty, actually. I'm making amendments to the menu which will give cook hysterics.'

Dorcas had never seen Juana, the Ruiz's cook, in any mood other than smiling complacency. She couldn't imagine her ever getting into a flap. But in case there was a side to Juana she hadn't seen, Dorcas offered: 'Would you like me to hang on? Perhaps Juana will require something extra fetching from the shops.'

'Even I dare not make such drastic changes on the day. No, Juana will have the ingredients. It is the commodity you can't buy she will be screaming for: time. So stop frittering it away. Go for your walk and take your distracting influence with you.'

Rose Ruiz's happy, chatty type of scolding took Dorcas down from the uncomfortable pedestal of revered guest and for the first time

128

she felt—oh—absurdly—but she felt that in being banished, she was at last being accepted.

Tears began to prickle behind her eyes. 'Thank you, señora,' she said rather stupidly.

Swallowing on something of an equally absurd nature, perhaps, Rose Ruiz said brightly: 'Just remember, with your fair skin, a sun hat is more than a decorative accessory.'

Waving a laughing goodbye, Dorcas dutifully went back upstairs to collect her sun hat before setting off. With its wide straw brim framing her face, it was neither intent nor coincidence, but something midway between the two, that turned her in the direction of the garage belonging to Tom Bennett, the friendly Englishman with whom she'd left her hired car. Only when she was well on her way did it occur to her that it had been in her mind for some time to enquire if he'd been adequately compensated for his trouble in towing the car into his garage and contacting the car hire firm. If the firm she'd hired the car from hadn't come up with a refund, and she didn't know of any clause in the car hire terms that said her claim was valid, then she ought to pay Tom Bennett for his services.

The road curved like a dusty whip. The sun-parched ground bore little evidence of the rain that had caused havoc and landslips. A walnut-faced Spaniard was digging a channel in the endless task of irrigating his land. He paused to shout a greeting to her as she passed. His greeting would have been just as friendly had she been a man, but his eyes appreciated the fact that she was a woman. The breeze teased the brim of her hat and softly slapped her cheeks. The sun ruled in solitary splendour, with not one attendant cloud in the vast sky kingdom.

Although her injured limb had stood up well, it was beginning to pain a little by the time she arrived at the *Garage Inglés.*

'Er . . . Mr Bennett? Tom?' she enquired of the jean-clad legs sticking out from beneath a car.

Sliding out, as tall and wide-grinned as she remembered him, Tom Bennett stuck an unmistakably oily hand through his pale yellow hair, like blanched maize in colour, and said: 'Miss West? Dorcas?' Confirming her last name and requesting permission to use her first.

'Yes.' Giving that permission. 'What a memory!'

'Ah well! What is easy on the eye is easy on the memory also. Don't you find?' he teased speculatively.

Matching his dry humour, she smiled up at him. 'You wouldn't by any chance be referring to the fact that I remembered your name?'

'Would I!' Despite the dark gleam in his eye, it was fun talk, quite devoid of undercurrents.

'I prefer to reserve judgement about that,'

she replied lightly.

Dorcas hadn't realized the amount of tension she'd been living under until she felt it begin to lift off. This happy sparring was just what she needed, to be able to talk to someone and—yes—flirt with them just a little without first weighing up the consequences of her actions and having to measure her every word. It was like rain to a thirsting flower to be able to look, talk, feel unimpeded by the shackles of circumstance.

'There's some beer in the house,' Tom said, jerking a square chin at the two-storey dwelling beyond the garage. 'What do you say if I clean up and . . .'

'I couldn't break you off from your work,' conscience made her protest, but not very convincingly and with hopeful eyes.

'You wouldn't be. I was just on the point of cleaning up anyway, to make a phone call. Of course, if you don't have the time to spare . . .?'

A bubble of hysteria rose in her throat. 'You don't know how funny that is. I've so much time I don't know what to do with it.'

Dorcas tried to maintain a smoothness of step as they walked towards the house, but she did not quite achieve this. Tom Bennett's glance acknowledged that he had noticed her limp, although he did not comment on it.

'Here we are—' Pushing open the door and allowing her to precede him into a low-ceilinged, but pleasantly light room. Although furnished in the Spanish style, Tom Bennett didn't follow the Spanish custom of shutting out the light, and sun motes played on the high-backed chair he directed her into.

'Relax. I'll just wash these.' Displaying his hands. 'Be back in a minute.' With that he disappeared into a room beyond, which was presumably the kitchen.

The splash of water as he washed his hands was oddly soothing. Obviously he'd included his face and hair as well, because he returned with his face clean and shining and his hair standing up in spikes after a vigorous towel rubbing.

He finger-smoothed his hair. In the way of a not very tidy man with no woman to pick things up after him, he said: 'I did have a comb somewhere.' Still grinning ruefully, he enquired: 'Can you hold out for that beer until I've made my phone call?'

'Of course. Is it a personal call? I don't mind going outside.'

But he was already moving towards the telephone which she had spotted on the writing desk in the corner. 'No . . . no. It's purely business.'

The writing desk resembled a box on legs. Its front flap was beautifully inlaid with Moorish motifs. Let down it provided a writing surface, and also revealed a complexity of drawers.

132

Tom Bennett opened three of these drawers before he found what he wanted, a scrap of not very clean paper bearing a telephone number.

'It's a client I have to phone to tell him his car is ready. A Señor Alfonso Roca. Perhaps you know him?' As Tom spoke he was already dialling for the operator. Simultaneously as he gave the number he wanted, Dorcas nodded to affirm that she was acquainted with Señor Roca.

A short while later, Tom set the receiver down. 'Señor Roca is sending his side-kick round to collect his car—Paco Garcia— perhaps you know him too? No?' Answering the brief shake of Dorcas's head. 'He's a handsome *hombre*. Ambitious but nice with it, if you know what I mean. Now . . . that beer. Unless you'd prefer coffee?'

Anticipating which he preferred, Dorcas said not quite truthfully: 'Beer sounds delightful.'

It came ice-cold from the fridge, misting up the glass, with a bitter yet refreshing taste. Dorcas hadn't known beer could taste so good.

Setting down his empty glass, Tom Bennett said casually: 'I don't remember that limp first time round, so I take it it's a recent acquisition. Come to think of it, there was talk you'd hurt your leg pretty badly.'

'It's better now, or nearly so. I only limped because I'd walked a long way.'

'As I heard it you came a cropper while assisting Enrique Ruiz's daughter and granddaughter when the train ran into trouble.'

'Did you?' she said with warding off coolness.

Nothing daunted, he continued smoothly: 'And as a result of this you are now staying with the extremely wealthy and infinitely grateful Señores Ruiz. Well, that figures.'

'What do you mean?' Her slow and distinct speech served to accentuate her anger.

'You've no cause to get prickly,' he said, sliding her a glance of reproof tempered with understanding. 'I wasn't inferring anything of a—well—devious nature, if that's what you're getting upset about. I meant it figured because the Ruizs have the reputation of being jolly nice people who are noted for their hospitality.'

'It seems that I have misunderstood you and I am sorry,' said a suitably contrite Dorcas.

'I should think so! As I see it, you were on hand to lend assistance to a couple of chicks the old señor happens to be mighty fond of, and so what more obvious than wanting to reward—'

'But that's just what I don't want,' Dorcas cut in hastily. 'I don't want rewarding.' To her horror, the culmination of her frustration found release in a large tear that squeezed past the trap of her hastily closed eyelids and slid helplessly down her cheek. 'I'm sorry for making such a spectacle of myself,' she gulped, 'but Michael's full of this talk about my receiving just reward and suitable compensation and I can't . . .' hiccup . . . 'stop him either. And it makes me feel so mercenary. I can't seem to get through to anybody that when I moved to help Feli and her baby, I wasn't activated by the hope of a reward.'

Tom was down on his haunches beside her, his face level with hers. 'Of course you weren't, honey. When you moved you didn't think, this is going to bring financial gain. You moved without thought, by instinct, to save a life—two lives—and I'm with Michael all the way in thinking you should derive some benefit. Who is this Michael, by the way?'

'My brother. He was touring France when I . . . when it happened. Señor Ruiz had him located through the authorities and now he's also a guest at the villa.'

'Humph! I'm glad. Glad you've got somebody to safeguard your interests because obviously you. . . you . . .'

Afterwards, Dorcas could never be sure which of them moved first. Her head found contact with his shoulder. She reasoned it out later that she lifted her chin to look at him just as he was bending to kiss the top of her head and by directing her mouth a fraction to the right—so she must accept the larger proportion of the blame—their lips met.

The seeking lightness of the enquiry in her lips was overwhelmed by the hunger in his. He kissed her as if to appease months of restraint. His mouth was on fire, but it could not ignite the smallest flame of feeling in her.

She knew—and she felt none too good about this—that she had deliberately invited—enticed!—his kiss, hoping it would blot out thoughts of Carlos. But . . . to feel nothing! To be kissed by this tall, fair giant, this blue-eyed beefcake, and feel nothing! Nothing that is, but a cold sickness of fear and apprehension inside; and the hollowed-out knowledge that nobody was ever going to eclipse Carlos.

It would have been so much easier all the way round if she could have transferred her affections. Carlos had shown superior wisdom when he said, 'I have sufficient sense to distrust the easy solution.' Well, she had proved she lacked sense, and her inept bungling must make reparation. She owed Tom an apology.

'I'm sorry.'

Those were the words she intended to say, but she did not speak them. Neither had they come from Tom's lips, which were still in the bemused trance of that kiss.

'There was no sign of you in the garage,' the voice continued, 'so I decided to try the house. The door was open. I am sorry. I did not mean to intrude on such a private moment. Señorita, my *amigo* Tom, what can I say but that I am devastated.'

Tom was the first to gain his wits. 'It's I who owe you an apology, don Paco. I knew you were coming. I should have been waiting in the forecourt with the keys of Señor Roca's car.'

'*Amigo*, I well understand.' Paco Garcia's eyes—brown depths of mischief—rested on Dorcas in such amused indulgence that she did not know where to look.

The colour swept into her cheeks and out again as she steeled herself for the inevitable introduction.

Seeing her embarrassment, Tom decided against this formality. 'The car keys are in the garage office, if you care to accompany me,' he said easily, and just as effortlessly conducted the charming, roguish faced don Paco out of the door.

In a way, she knew why she'd done it. Carlos was the first. She had no past experiences to draw on, no way of testing her feelings.

Dorcas waited listlessly for Tom to come back, the apology and explanation—if she could explain this away—still to be made.

She told herself it was normal to feel uneasy when faced with so unenviable a task, and that don Paco would quickly forget something of so little importance. As Alfonso's right-hand man, don Paco would be acquainted with Carlos. Don Paco was a man of the world; he wouldn't gossip about something as trivial as a kiss. Would he?

*   *   *

'Sorry about that,' said Tom on his return. But Dorcas saw, with deepening consternation, that he didn't look sorry at all. On the contrary, he looked smug, as if life had given him a much-wanted lift.

Dorcas flung about in her mind for the words to bring him down to earth, but in such a way as not to deflate his ego. The stark words were readily available, it was the tactful ones that were proving difficult to collect.

But when Tom took hold of her hand and made to draw her in his arms again, with every appearance of continuing from where he had left off, her instinctive cringing back was more cruel than the most blunt, unglossed by kindness truth her tongue could have conveyed.

He started back, as if the hand raised to stem the cry of dismay on her lips had come down hard on his cheek. He had a slapped-down look that made Dorcas ache inside.

'I'm so sorry, Tom. I shouldn't have led you on.'

'Presumably you had your reasons,' he said with commendable restraint.

'Yes. I was . . . sort of testing my feelings. I hoped you could make me forget someone else. And please don't take it personally that

138

you didn't.'

In concentrating on his expression, Dorcas had forgotten to guard her own. When she remembered, it was too late. She wondered how sick she looked when the sympathy she should have given him was bestowed upon her.

'I'm sorry the experiment was such a success,' he said in the kindest, most sincere voice she had ever heard.

'What do you mean? A success? Shouldn't that be failure?' Her guilt gave way to perplexity.

'Whatever you care to call it, it obviously proved a depth of feeling it would have been more convenient not to own.'

His sympathetic perception—hardly a male characteristic and rarely found to this point of understanding in females—left her gasping.

When he said: 'I'm right, aren't I?' she could only nod in dumb agreement as the silly, weak tears threatened to press under her eyelids again.

'Will you believe that I'm not really a crying sort of person? It's just that you seem to understand so well.'

His mouth wavered on the edge of a bleak smile. 'By what conceit do you think you have the prerogative to give your heart foolishly!'

'*Tom*,' she said with feeling. 'You too? That makes it even worse. I feel awful for using you.'

His expression searched hers. He seemed to

be swallowing on a decision. 'All right, I can't let you go on thinking you are the only one who is put to shame. I see I'll have to own up. While you were using me, you served a very useful purpose.'

'I don't know what you mean.'

'Well,' he began stumblingly, 'it's a pretty brutal admission to make, but the tru—' He bit that sharply off and made practical use of the 'th' trembling on his tongue. '*That* is to say, I was practising on you. I haven't been keeping my hand in and . . . well . . . when Jane arrives I don't want her to think that she's come all the way from England to marry an oaf who's forgotten how to kiss a girl.'

'Jane . . . from England . . . to marry . . .? Oh, Tom, I'm so pleased. You don't know what a relief this is. When?'

'When?' he repeated blankly, his face going through a series of expressions with one common factor: guilt.

She told him laughingly: 'You don't need to look so agitated. I forgive you for kissing me to keep in practise. Men have committed greater crimes than that without turning a hair. When is your girl arriving?'

'Er . . . tomorrow.' His eyes skidded to the envelope propped against the fruit bowl on the side table. 'Jane is due to arrive tomorrow,' he said with greater conviction, 'barring delays, of course. If it isn't the ground staff threatening industrial action, it's the air hostesses

140

complaining about snagging their tights.'

Dorcas decided he was adopting this light, comic approach to contain his excitement. 'How long is it since you last met?'

'Three very heavy years,' he said, proving her surmise right. He suddenly began to talk quite naturally. 'It was a classroom romance that grew as we did. She went to work in a local bank, and I served my time in a garage, accruing knowledge and saving as hard as I could. By the time I'd saved enough to open up my own place, on a modest scale mind, just a few pumps, it was no longer a practical proposition. The Arabs wanted more out of the deal, the government was putting the screw on. If that wasn't enough to put me off, the giants of the industry were swallowing all the little men up. Instead of dropping my ambition, it began to take on a new perspective. I'd always dreamed of breaking away to a new country. Why not now? The more I thought about it, the more I liked it. I talked it over with Jane and between us we decided on Spain. Let's face it, we hadn't the money to start up in a more expensive country. The preparations we had to make— everything—just flowed. It was so easy it was unbelievable. I remember thinking it was too easy. Nothing in this world ever goes quite so smoothly to plan as things were going for us. But I was wrong in looking for a small hitch. When it came it was a big one that nearly put paid to the whole idea. At the eleventh hour, Jane's mother took ill. Jane made me see that she had to stay and see her mother back in good health, and then she set about persuading me to come out by myself. At first I didn't want to, but then I saw that perhaps this was the best way. I could find out the lay of the land, get established, make a home for her.' His voice seemed to trail down, finishing on a note of dejection. Perhaps he didn't think he'd done as well as he ought to have done.

'Well you have,' Dorcas said robustly. 'You've got an established garage and a home that any girl would be proud to come to.'

'Do you think so? You're not just saying that to be polite? You really mean it?'

'Of course I do,' she said, touched by his eager reaction to her words of praise.

'Not knowing much about these things,' he explained, 'whenever I went to buy anything for the home, I tried to look at it through Jane's eyes. You can't know what a relief it is—' His eyes went blank, as if he'd just remembered something.

'And you'll see that you have,' said Dorcas, 'when Jane looks round and tells you it is exactly how she pictured it.'

'Yes,' he said. 'Yes of course.' But he was speaking in that funny, false voice again.

'Tom? Is anything the matter?'

'What could be the matter?' he countered. 'Come to that, now that all is explained and you have been expiated of guilt, why aren't you looking more chirpy?'

'There is something,' she admitted. 'It's not the fact that we kissed that's troubling me. It's that we were seen. Do you think Señor Garcia will tell?'

'Tell who?'

'Well, he could tell Jane.'

'That is very unlikely,' Tom retorted drily.

'You're right,' Dorcas said blissfully. 'He would hardly gossip about that to your fiancée. But—' frowning again '—He might gossip to someone else. If it were to reach Señora Ruiz's ears, she wouldn't think much of her house guest, would she?'

'You do mean *Señora* Ruiz?' Tom said speculatively. 'I seem to remember the señora has a rather handsome son.'

Dorcas's blush not only answered that, but supplied the possible identity of the man she'd kissed him to forget.

'Good grief!' he said. As he wasn't such an egomaniac as to believe he could make anybody forget Carlos Ruiz, he found himself swallowing back his own wry smile. 'You didn't ask much of me! In a way, though, I suppose you've paid me a tremendous compliment.' On this benign thought he said kindly: 'Don't worry, I know just the word to say to don Paco to ensure he doesn't tell . . . *Señora* Ruiz.'

143

CHAPTER SEVEN

The pause, the emphasis Tom gave to Señora Ruiz's name was very revealing. Tom had guessed it was Carlos she didn't want to know, because it was Carlos she loved. She wasn't so much bothered that Tom knew, but she was shocked that she was so transparent that even a stranger could read her. And yet Tom didn't seem like a stranger.

His eyes moved to her from their preoccupation with the letter propped against the fruit bowl, and it occurred to her that he should be more excited at the prospect of his fiancée's arrival next day. In his shoes, she would be hitting the ceiling. It just served to prove that Tom had a better clamp on his emotions than she had. This thought carried with it more than a slight trace of envy. It would be nice to have the cover of glass, of the shatter-proof variety, without its see-through qualities.

Tom brought her out of her reverie by saying: 'Come on, nuisance. I'll run you back.'

'Am I? A nuisance?' She certainly seemed to be one all the way round.

'No. It was just something to say. I didn't mean it.'

'Do you often say things you don't mean?'

'Not often. Dorcas, if I wasn't crazy about

Jane and if you weren't crazy about this *hombre* you kissed me to forget, there would be a chance for us.'

'Go on with you. It's just something to say again.'

'No.' His hands cupped her face. 'If Jane jilts me, and if things don't work out for you and your guy, will you marry me?'

It would be a miracle if things did work out for her and Carlos, but Jane must know she had pure gold in Tom. Dorcas could give an affirmative reply in the absolute certainty that it could never come to pass.

'Given those circumstances, yes Tom, I will marry you.' They should both have laughed then, only they didn't. Dorcas's throat was curiously tight.

'Will you please excuse me while I have an emotional freak-out. I'm not used to proposals. Even insincere ones.'

'What makes you think that one was insincere? I meant every word, Dorcas. That makes it sincere.'

'Within the context of the wording,' she put in hastily. 'Yes. Within the context of the wording.'

His serious features were transformed by his quick, sweet smile, witnessed previously during the morning, but never before with quite this impact. And she saw what he meant about the sincerity bit because she thought, if I weren't hooked on Carlos, and you didn't have Jane, I could fall for you in a big way.

'Another beer before I take you back?'

Dorcas couldn't remember drinking the first one. She had abandoned her glass somewhere while it was still half full.

'I would rather not. To tell you the truth I'm feeling a bit weary, and I suspect that's how I look. If you really mean it about giving me a lift, I'd like to go now please, and then I'll have time to tidy up before lunch. Are you quite sure you can spare the time?'

'Quite sure.'

In a matter of minutes she was seated beside him in his car. The return journey was accomplished in a fraction of the time it had taken her to walk it. Thinking of that walk, along that very dusty track, made her look down at her bare, sandalled feet. They were deplorably dirty. Not only that but her hair— the unflattering consequence of wearing a sun hat in fierce heat—was flattened to her head in perspiring tendrils. She thought it little wonder that Tom hadn't contradicted her when she said she thought she must look weary.

As Tom would have pulled up at the curly wrought-iron main gate, she said: 'Will you drive round, please. There's a small side gate. Could you drop me there, please. I've just remembered that my hostess is expecting visitors for lunch. I don't want to be caught looking the sight I do and there's always at least one early arrival.'

Tom followed her instructions, and in doing so also followed the course of a long black car. He said: 'Do you think someone else is choosing to sneak in without being seen?'

Both cars pulled up at the same gate.

'It would appear so,' said Dorcas, recognizing the car. 'It's Señor Ruiz. Would you like to meet him?'

'I think I'd better,' said Tom, killing the engine. 'It might look odd if I just drove off.'

Enrique Ruiz had a marked twinkle in his eye as he approached Dorcas and Tom. Addressing Dorcas he said: 'Do I have a guilty accomplice?'

'I just remembered the señora is expecting guests for lunch. I thought I should make myself presentable before joining them.'

'I also remembered. I, too, like to prepare myself for the ordeal of meeting my wife's women friends. But I prefer liquid fortification. This way is a short-cut to my study. Perhaps you and your friend would care to join me?'

'I'm so sorry,' said Dorcas, realizing she had been remiss over the introductions. 'Señor, may I introduce Tom Bennett. Tom is the owner of the *Garage Inglés.*'

'I am aware of that,' said Enrique Ruiz, 'although we have not previously met. I have heard good reports of your work. You are gaining the reputation of being a first class

147

mechanic. I have been meaning to put some business your way for some time. I will do so without delay.'

'Thank you, sir. You are very kind.'

'I am a business man. Kindness does not come into it. Now quickly, into my study,' Enrique Ruiz said with such brisk authority that neither Dorcas nor Tom dare do other than obey.

'Is white rum to your taste, young man?'

Tom said it was. Then Señor Ruiz said: 'White rum is not for little girls. A light *fino* is a more fitting apéritif for you, Dorcas.'

The señor handed Dorcas her sherry. As she watched him pour white rum generously into two glasses, she thought that if her kind señor had a heart complaint, he too would have been wiser to choose the sherry. She wondered if the señora knew her husband drank spirits before lunch.

'Dorcas is looking at me in a most disapproving way,' the señor said naughtily. 'Save that look, Dorcas. You will need it when you are a wife.'

'Not if she marries me,' Tom stated, with equal wickedness. 'I won't do anything that Dorcas disapproves of.'

'Is such a union possible?' don Enrique enquired with obvious interest, and if it hadn't been a fanciful notion, Dorcas would have thought his curiosity was spiced with dismay.

Tom gave a very definite and succinct yes.

Dorcas took longer over her reply, wording carefully because she wanted to be sure that nothing could be misinterpreted, nothing misunderstood.

'Tom proposed that in the unlikely event of our being free of present emotional encumberments, we should marry each other. Keeping scrupulously to that wording, I said yes.'

In the face of don Enrique's bewilderment, Dorcas struggled on. 'It is the sort of promise that is never taken up. Like a small daughter saying she is going to marry her papa when she grows up.'

Were small Spanish girls too sensible to make such a statement? Just as Dorcas was beginning to despair, comprehension lit the deceptively austere Latin features.

'Ah . . . you funny English! I now have the understanding. Please have the patience with a dull old man. I am over thirty years into a marriage with an English woman and yet a turn of phrase, a piece of humour that is peculiarly English, still baffles me.' Enrique Ruiz had the most kindly penetrating eyes of any man she knew. Dorcas saw a smile creep into their expression. 'I am not, as you English say, "with it".'

Predictably, don Enrique invited Tom to stay to lunch. 'I am not asking because when the hour reaches so, it is only polite to ask a visitor to stay. I am asking you to honour my

149

table for a purely selfish reason. I do not care to be the only male lunching with the women's sewing circle.'

'Doesn't Michael intend being in for lunch?' Dorcas asked.

'Sadly no. Your brother is absent on some business of his own.' Indicating what he thought was the nature of that business, he patted the portion of his chest where he judged his heart to be.

Dorcas let it bounce off her. At the moment she could do without thoughts of Michael's amorous antics, her own being all the weight her mind could take.

'You haven't met Señorita West's charming brother?' Enrique Ruiz enquired of Tom.

Tom admitted that he had not had that pleasure.

Enrique Ruiz seemed to chuckle over Tom's choice of words. 'A pleasure . . . yes. For the ladies and still a pleasure for me because I do not enjoy the limelight and I do not mind that Michael steals this for himself. As Michael is not to be present at lunch, I look for an ally.'

'I appreciate the invitation, Señor Ruiz, but I must say no. It's not that I'm daunted by the matrons of the women's sewing circle—well, not all that much—but I really must get back to my work. I'm already behind on my schedule.'

'And you can't put off while tomorrow? No, it is not right that I should ask.'

'Tomorrow is a big day for Tom,' Dorcas said importantly. 'His fiancée is arriving from England.'

'In that case I will not attempt to persuade you to stay. Perhaps some other time.'

'I shall look forward to it, señor.'

'It has been good meeting you, my boy. I will not forget my promise to put some business your way. It is not a favour. Your work merits it.'

'It is kind of you, señor. I shall be most grateful. Thank you for your hospitality.'

The final goodbyes were said. Tom went. Dorcas would have gone too, already too many minutes had been shaven off her getting-ready-for-lunch time, but don Enrique put out a detaining hand.

'Tom Bennett is a very nice, a very pleasant young man, but I am glad he has a fiancée who is arriving from England tomorrow. I am not saying he would not make you a fine husband, because he probably would; what I am saying is that I do not want to lose you. Not just yet.' A question was vaguely surfacing in his eyes. The smile that was so like Carlos's quivered across his features, a smile of such inveigling charm that Dorcas would willingly have told him whatever he wanted to know. 'You said both you and Señor Bennett had emotional encumberments.'

So that was what he wanted to know. It was the one thing Dorcas dare not tell him. She knew he was fond of her. She did not want to put that affection at risk by naming his son as the man she loved.

The slamming of a car door, heralding the arrival of the first guest, saved Dorcas the necessity of answering.

'We will talk later, child. If you hurry you will not be caught.'

Now that the noose was no longer straining round her neck, Dorcas could smile.

'Wish me luck, señor. Although a pair of wings on my heels would be of more practical use.'

*   *   *

Dorcas thought about what to wear while she was under the shower. Her choice, a crisp, glazed cotton shirtwaister, suited a fresh, unmade-up face. She had time only to apply moisturizer and lipstick. A quick comb through her hair, a fresh pair of sandals located and put on, and she was ready to face Rose Ruiz's guests. Maria Roca, Isabel's mama, represented the only familiar face. It meant a gruelling session of introductions before she could take her place at the dining table.

Mercifully, she found herself next to Señora Roca, who took the first opportunity to whisper: 'They are not as formidable as they look. I must warn you, though, to expect a

152

barrage of questions. When women reach a certain age of maturity, curiosity takes second place to tact.'

'Thank you, señora. I will bear that in mind.' For what good it would do her. 'Is Isabel not with you today?' Allowing outlet to her own curiosity.

'The naughty child made prior arrangements. I see your brother is absent too.'

'Señor Ruiz suspects Michael of having a romantic assignation.'

The moment the words were out, Dorcas knew she'd blundered. But Señora Roca didn't pick her up, which made her wonder if she wasn't being too mentally alert. It could be coincidental that Isabel Roca *and* Michael weren't present.

But now that the idea had sparked, it wouldn't go away. Michael was meeting someone in secret. Right from the start Isabel had drooled openly over him, and Michael was rat enough to take an unfair advantage of Isabel's infatuation. Perhaps she was doing Michael an injustice in piling all the blame on him because Isabel would be difficult to resist. She was a beauty; despite her air of girlish innocence, she had the full appeal of a woman.

'Is anything the matter, child?' Maria Roca asked anxiously.

'I hope not,' said Dorcas. 'I sincerely hope not.'

153

'Carlos got off all right this morning?' Señora Roca enquired guilelessly, although she had said the one name guaranteed to rivet Dorcas's attention. 'Such a dear boy. The man he has become reflects the child he was. Always polite and well mannered. By that I do not mean he was a quiet child. Dear me, no! Just the opposite. I could tell you some of his pranks . . .' And Maria Roca did just that until the matron on the other side, making it clear she thought Dorcas had been monopolized long enough, decided it was time she had a slice of her attention.

* * *

For the rest of the day Dorcas kept an eye open for Michael's return, but although it was now evening, she still had not seen him. Sooner or later, and instinct pressed for later, she was going to have to have things out with him. There was still the business of his having told that exaggerated story of her not being able to follow a brilliant career because of the injury to her leg. Even though he had done no apparent damage, he must have known he was going against her wishes. And now there was this new fear that Michael was playing fast and loose with Isabel Roca. Couldn't he see the danger? Didn't he appreciate that this wasn't England?

Even as Dorcas built herself up to give

Michael the cautionary telling off she felt he so justly deserved, she anticipated the outcome with a weary sort of inevitability. Michael had a way of manipulating words to suit his own ends that was little short of genius. She had the strongest feeling that his plausible tongue would make his wrong-doing sound like an act of gallantry. So many times she had started off knowing she was right, but had found herself being turned round until she was agreeing with Michael.

During the day the sun blanched this part of the terrace, draining the flowers of their scents and weighting the air with an exotic blend of fragrances that was overpowering. Evening was kinder. The breeze that gentled the flowers carried a fainter and more subtle scent. The tranquillity of her surroundings smoothed away her frown. It was sacrilege to let all this be spoilt for her by thoughts of Michael. But the line between having the conviction and following it is perilously thin. Dorcas did not manage to tread it very successfully, because her thoughts kept returning to her brother's cavalier attitude to life.

The interruption would have been welcome on its own account. The content of it made it doubly so.

'Teléfono, señorita.'

Dorcas looked up to see Teresa standing before her. Who would be telephoning her?

'Are you sure it's for me?' she asked the

155

little Spanish maid.

'*Sí* señorita.'

Behind the respectfully straight mouth was a look that Dorcas could not immediately identify. The caller—male, if Dorcas correctly read the delighted interest Teresa was so valiantly trying to suppress—was someone Teresa knew.

'Hurry, señorita,' Teresa implored, adding a further clue. Someone whose orders Teresa was conditioned to carry out at speed.

Not someone: Carlos? Yes? Her heart did its usual high vault, and the stuffing that seemed to have come out of her legs filled her mouth with a cotton wool effect.

'Teresa, is it—' And Dorcas stopped. It seemed blatantly revealing to ask Teresa if it was Carlos, with such bright hope in her eyes.

'*Sí*, señorita, it is the young señor,' said Teresa, not noticing that Dorcas had omitted to say his name.

Dorcas breathed on relief when Teresa indicated the telephone in the hall. It would have been too inhibiting to have to take the call on the drawing room extension with Rose Ruiz listening. Even so, the hall, with its many doors leading off, was not exactly private. She must keep this fact in mind.

'Hello, Dorcas here,' she said in a voice that did not live up to her good intention by failing to hide all the strange things going on inside her.

His delighted laugh underlined her negative attempt. 'It is Carlos here, as you are already aware.' Implying, pompously, that she only went to pieces for him.

'Good evening, Carlos,' she said with exaggerated correctness. 'Did you have a safe and pleasant journey?'

'A safe journey, yes. It was not pleasant to leave you.'

She refused to be put off by the teasing reproach in his voice, and persisted: 'Have you got a nice room?'

'I have been given the room I am always given when I stay at this particular hotel. It is on the seventh floor, where it is quiet.'

'If you are away from the noise, you will be able to work undisturbed.'

'That is the general idea. Always before I have been able to write out my notes. This time I am distracted by thoughts of you.'

'If you are on the seventh floor,' she said, wildly searching her brain for the words to switch the content of the conversation to something of a more manageable, less explosive content, 'you must have a magnificent view.'

'The hotel is situated on the highest point and is renowned for its view. The daytime impression from my balcony is of a higgledy-piggledy series of drops. It gives an avalanche effect of building sitting upon building. Church standing upon tall slim apartment block,

157

municipal building standing upon church. The city is overflowing with people; the roads are chronically blocked by cars. By day the sun strikes with malice. The evening is reward for sustaining the day. The city lights come on one by one. The places of special interest, the cathedral, the parks and gardens and some of the more distinguished monuments, are illuminated. I wish you could see my view by night. I think you would agree it is almost perfect.'

'*Almost* perfect. From the way you have described it to me, I know if I were there I should think it quite perfect.'

'If you were here it would be. My view is not perfect because I cannot see you.'

'You are not being fair, Carlos. I am trying to remain very cool and level-headed, and you are not helping me one little bit.'

'Why should I? I do not want you cool and level-headed.'

His voice, stripped of everything but that soft, seductive note, grated on feelings that were too newly exposed to be anything but raw and tender. She was glad he could not see the blush in her cheeks, marking her weakness and vulnerability. She clutched the telephone mouthpiece harder to stop it dancing up and down in her shaking fingers.

'Carlos, *please.*' Besides the passionate plea in her voice there was a note of censure that contrasted sharply with the aching longing in her to hear more. 'Carlos?' she said into the small silence that followed.

'I am thinking up insincere words of contrition. Do I apologize for speaking the truth?'

'I do not know what the truth is,' she said distractedly—in desperation.

'I could say I'm not prepared to tell you over the telephone, but I suspect I do so every time I open my mouth.'

She could tell by the tone of his voice that his face had relaxed into gentleness.

'Carlos, I'm so confused. I don't know what to believe . . .' Her voice tailed away tiredly. She felt emotionally drained.

'Just believe,' he said softly. 'And now, goodnight little one. *Buenas noches, pequeña,*' he repeated in Spanish.

'*Buenas noches.* Carlos—' urgently '—Don't ring off. You haven't told me why you phoned.'

'I phoned to say goodnight.'

'Oh . . . goodnight then, Carlos.'

'Goodnight, *cariña.*'

She replaced the receiver in a haze of joy. Carlos had said, just believe. Dare she believe that . . . believe that he . . . that he loved her?

'Are you all right, Dorcas?'

Dorcas answered in the abstracted daze she was in. 'No, señor. I don't think I will ever be all right again. Oh!'—as it hit her. 'Señor Ruiz! I spoke without thinking. Even though I heard you and even answered you, I did not properly

159

realize you were standing there.'

'I understand,' Enrique Ruiz said, stroking his beard reflectively. 'At least I think I understand. I would know I understood if I also knew the name of your caller. If, for instance, I knew your caller was male. What am I saying, of course your caller was male! Only a man could paint such joy on your face, eh, Dorcas?'

His smile burst into mischief. His curiosity, though impertinent, was of the kindly nature that Dorcas was not proof against. All this weighed in with the compulsion to tell someone, and it did not seem at all incongruous that this someone was Carlos's father.

'It was Carlos. He telephoned to say goodnight,' she said, in part triumph, and part disbelief.

The bearded chin nodded sagely. 'That is what I thought. You did not speak up clearly enough for me to know for certain that you spoke my son's name.'

'I am sorry, señor,'—straight-mouthed. 'Next time I will speak loud enough for you to hear.'

Unabashed, her kind señor said: 'Next time it might be wiser to take the call in the privacy of my study. 'It might also be wiser—' Taking Dorcas's arm and guiding her feet across the hall—'if we continue this conversation with due regard to privacy. Come into my study for a moment.'

He did not speak again until they were in that masculine, book-lined room. Taking p ride of place on his desk was a silver framed photograph of Rose Ruiz. Beside it, appropriately, in a crystal vase, was a rose. The scent of this perfect bloom filled the room like an overpowering presence. Dorcas felt the potency of Rose Ruiz's dominant personality as though the señora was standing by her side.

Enrique Ruiz also felt the domination of the rose—which was cut at the peak of its perfection and changed daily—but in a different way. His fingers brushed against the petals, absorbing the sweetness into his fingertips, and the eyes of an old man glazed over with the love of a young boy.

His chin came up. Without preamble he said: 'Let us not shadow box, Dorcas. Let us come out in the open. Has Carlos said anything to you?'

'If I replied that Carlos has said many things to me, would I be shadow boxing?'

'Yes, Dorcas.'

'Very well. Carlos has not asked me to marry him. But he has given me to believe that he will do so on his return.'

'It is exactly as I thought,' he said with disarming candour.

'You are not displeased, señor?'

'That does not come into it.'

'What does, señor?'

161

'I think you have been a part of our household long enough to appreciate the obstacles.'

'Do you mean the señora?' As far as Dorcas could see, Rose Ruiz loomed over her as the biggest obstacle.

'My wife is not an obstacle,' he chided, but more in humour than rebuke. 'She is the finger pointing out the obstacle.'

'I'm sorry, señor. I shouldn't have made that unkind reference. Señora Ruiz has shown me every kindness.' Her voice melted to nothing.

'Your shame and your honesty do you credit, *niñas*. But let us not digress. Carlos already has a *novia*.

'Isabel Roca.' Dorcas supplied the name with dignity, keeping the twist of jealousy well hidden beneath a matter-of-fact tone.

'As you say, Isabel Roca has long been my son's sweetheart. A marriage between them would ally a long-standing friendship and cement a business merger that is imperative for the survival of both families. I will not go into the details because I know you are already acquainted with them.' At Dorcas's involuntary start, his face bent a question at her. 'Does it surprise you so much that my wife informed me of the—' a delicate pause '—small conversation she had with you on the subject of why Carlos should marry the daughter of our dear friends?'

'Yes it does. I would have thought she'd

keep that to herself.' The truth pumped out of Dorcas. Too late she realized where her unfortunate honesty was leading her. 'Oh, I'm sorry! I didn't mean to criticize the señora's actions. After all, it's natural for a mother to warn off . . .' If, when she had made her first slip, she had left it there, it wouldn't have been too bad. She was making it worse by going on about it.

Dorcas realized there was something odd in the way Enrique Ruiz was looking at her. It did not prepare her. Having sustained one shock, she was ripe for the next.

'It is true that my wife endeavoured to warn you off.' His eyes pierced hers with a brilliance of meaning. 'On whose behalf do you think she was acting?'

So the señora wasn't against her. She had been merely carrying out someone else's instructions.

'Yours, señor?' she said. She had to grapple with the dizziness in her brain to think.

Nothing had changed. He wasn't coming down heavily against her because . . . But the because of it evaded her. She wasn't forgetting about the business angle. It would be a happy solution if Carlos were to marry Isabel Roca, but the feeling persisted that it went deeper than that. There was something else. But what?

She considered the options open to her. She could ask Enrique Ruiz to tell her now, or she could leave it until Carlos returned and ask him to explain it to her. Providing, of course, he knew.

Enrique Ruiz began to speak in a curiously sad-happy tone that blended well with the expression on his face. 'It is true, you know.'

'What is, señor?'

'Life's strange continuity. If you live long enough, the past catches up with you.'

'What are you talking about, señor?'

'You have been unwise enough to awaken certain aspects of the past, and so invite the nostalgic ramblings of an old man. Seeing you and Carlos together, observing the way you exchange glances when you think no one is looking, is like seeing a memory replayed. It has made me feel young again, but at the same time I have not been given youth's energy to fight. I fought last time. Oh, how I fought last time! I cannot go through all that again. You have no idea at all what I am talking about, have you?'

'No, señor.'

'In the short time I have known you, Dorcas, you have become very dear to me, but I must oppose any marriage between you and my son. If Carlos were to marry you, he would bring dishonour to the family name and near ruination to the family business. And this will be quite apart from the fact that a merger will no longer seem so desirable from my friend, don Alfonso's point of view. Long-standing

164

orders will be withdrawn as the expression of disapproval certain of our clients will feel it necessary to make. Carlos will have a hard task, he will need to drive himself to unendurable limits just to build the business back to its present strength—which as we have already agreed, is not sufficient for survival. So you see, Dorcas, you would not be enriching my son's life, but taking from it. I am sorry to appear so ruthless, but I must ask this question. Could you do this, Dorcas? Could you?'

'How can you be so certain it would be like this?' Dorcas pressed.

Instead of giving her an answer, he seemed to swerve from the main issue. And yet Dorcas got the feeling that this was keenly relevant.

'Nor can we discount your homesickness. My dear wife's eyes used to fill with such wistful longing merely by looking at a Constable painting. She said she could smell the grass, and this made her nostalgic for England.'

Of course! Dorcas saw the link and knew he wasn't talking at random. She didn't know the details of Enrique Ruiz's courtship of Rose, but thirty years ago a man of his standing would have been expected to marry into a Spanish house of equal social distinction. Had it been a disappointment, a scandal even, when he turned aside from tradition and chose an English bride who could not bring him

165

valuable business connections? And now the wheel had turned full circle.

Dorcas was so deep in thought that she did not notice the señor get up and go over to the wine cabinet. She blinked in some surprise at the brandy goblet placed before her. Brandy? She must look as sick as she felt.

'Is that to your taste?' Enrique Ruiz enquired, not unkindly.

Dorcas took a tentative sip. A cup of tea would have been infinitely preferable, but she nodded, wondering with a clutch of apprehension if tea wouldn't have served Enrique Ruiz better than the contents of his glass. Or did he too need the stimulus of brandy?

On some vague, not properly functioning plane of thought, it came to her that Carlos had entrusted her to see that stress was kept to minimal proportions, and yet here she was contributing to it. Yet the señor did not give the appearance of a man under stress. True, there was a tensile look about him, but it was an expression that pursued a happier, lighter element of thought which in her view did not fit under the heading of stress.

And then, of course, there was his benign manner towards her, lulling her into a false sense of security.

Nevertheless, she kept her eyes fixed fiercely on her brandy glass. 'You must think me very stupid, señor, not to have seen before

166

that this is parallel with a major event in your life. But—' She stopped and swallowed, tightly clasping her hands round her glass, as though to stop the conviction that she was right—and her daring in declaring this—from slipping away. 'Times have changed. You are speaking as though thirty years has been put under a glass case, untouched by a softening outlook that makes what was an outrage then, no more than something to gossip over now.'

Enrique Ruiz did not react; he neither expressed pleasure nor displeasure at Dorcas's spirited outburst, causing her to reflect, in self-doubt, that perhaps she had gone too far. Isabel Roca would never have spoken up in this way. Isabel Roca accepted the social system that put women subservient to men. But that structure of thought was too restrictive for someone of Dorcas's enlightened outlook. She was very much afraid that her kind señor saw her frankness as impertinence.

One moment Enrique Ruiz was pondering the curling, down-swept lashes that only screened, without totally hiding, the militant fire. The next he was being swept up in the apology issuing from eyes that were devoid of the light of argument. And while her look awarded him the veneration he had come to expect from someone of Dorcas's age, he sighed for that lost spark of rebellion.

When Dorcas said: 'I'm sorry, señor. For a

moment I forgot myself,' he was quick to reply: 'Your reaction was most predictable, my dear. I believe I used much the same words in reply to my father's opposition.'

Meeting his eyes, Dorcas did not know whether she had won or lost.

CHAPTER EIGHT

The following day the house was thrown into a state of uproar by the unheralded arrival of Madelena Ruiz, Carlos's imperious grandmother. She stepped out of a vintage taxi, a deceptively fragile-looking old lady with the bearing of a queen, and mounted the steps with the taxi driver in attendance.

While Brigida went to alert her master and mistress, Dorcas automatically pulled her stomach in, her shoulders back, and tweaked an offending wisp of hair into place behind her ear.

A process she saw repeated brief seconds later as Rose Ruiz advanced to greet her mother-in-law. Reverently taking those incredibly tiny hands in a warm, although slightly nerve-disorientated welcome, she said: 'Why didn't you let us know you were coming? Enrique could have fetched you to lessen the strain of the journey.'

Dark flashing eyes made their unhurried appraisal of Rose Ruiz's flushed features and rather harassed expression. Standing to one side, visible without making her presence blatantly obvious, Dorcas thought: 'You wicked old woman! Carlos's grandmother knew she was plunging her daughter-in-law into deep confusion; knew it and was revelling in it! It was strange, and not a little disturbing, to see Rose Ruiz's dominant personality crushed by this diminutive presence.

The old lady didn't so much speak as grant an audience. 'I have been well looked after,' she said, waving grandly in the direction of the taxi driver, who was hovering uncertainly, still clasping the pigskin suitcase. The suitcase provided only a limited clue. It was larger than an overnight stay would warrant, but not large enough for the requirements of a longer stay of say more than a week.

'Put the suitcase down,' *doña* Madelena instructed crisply, with little patience for the poor taxi driver's awe of her. 'Yes there. Rose, pay him.'

'Of course. Certainly.' By this time her husband had also put in an appearance. 'Enrique?' she appealed.

Enrique Ruiz paid off the taxi driver who bowed his head in polite homage at the assembly in general, before making his escape.

'It is good to see you,' Enrique Ruiz said, kissing his mother's offered cheek before holding her slight frame at a good viewing angle. He then proceeded to coax warmth into those cold, aristocratic features with the melting magnetism of his smile. 'You are looking wonderfully well, *Madre.*'

'Looks can be deceptive,' she said, sniffing autocratically, but succumbing to her son's charm with obvious enjoyment.

Dorcas was more than content to stay in the background, but knew it was only a matter of time before the old lady's compelling gaze swept her into the unwelcome limelight. It zoomed round the hall, focusing on her like a high-powered beam. The resonant voice boomed out: 'What are you doing skulking in the shadows? Come forward, child, and let me look at you.'

Dorcas went through the stomach in, shoulders back routine again, and for good measure added several deep swallows. She came forward, marvelling that such a fragile looking person could have so strong a voice and such an overwhelming personality.

Not quite knowing what to do, she said: '*Buenas tardes*, señora.' And held out her hand in a very formal, very English way. To her delight it was ignored in favour of her cheek, which received a paper cool kiss.

Dorcas was less delighted to hear the old señora's cruelly perceptive observation. 'You look better than when I last saw you, but not as well as you should look. What is bothering you? Is it your leg?'

'I do not know that anything is bothering me,' said Dorcas as a medium-sized flurry of unease threatened to wreck her insecure confidence. 'My leg is better. I have to return to the hospital in two weeks' time for a final examination. But that is just a formality.'

'Ah . . . yes. Formalities . . . rituals to be

observed.' Her stick impatiently tapped the mosaic tiles. 'The ritual of greeting has overrun its time. How long are you going to keep me standing here, Rose? Show me to my room.'

The redirection of attention allowed Dorcas to breathe easier.

Rose Ruiz sprang forward. 'Of course, *Madre*. How inconsiderate of me. Take my arm.'

The tapping of her silver-topped stick marked her painfully slow progress. As the old eyes flicked back at her, Dorcas knew she had only been awarded a temporary respite. It would all be wheedled out of her, but at the same time she knew she had a kindly inquisitor in Carlos's grandmother.

*   *   *

'. . . and there it is, señora,' Dorcas confided some hours later. The journey had tired the old matriarch more than she cared to admit. She had grudgingly concurred that . . . yes, perhaps she would have a supper tray in her room. Barely had Dorcas finished her coffee than the summons came that doña Madelena wished to see her before she retired for the night.

As she had known it would be, Dorcas had been in the grand presence a matter of minutes before the truth was prised out of her.

172

'I love Carlos, but how can he love me? I'm so ordinary. And even if he did love me, it would be hopeless.' All the time Dorcas was speaking she kept her eyes shyly fixed on her hands. 'And then, of course, there is Michael's attitude. You haven't met my brother yet, señora. He sends his regards and I am to tell you that he looks forward to seeing you in the morning. You'll like Michael, at least I think you will like him, because most people do. Unlike me, he always knows the right thing to say. Only, it always seems to be the wrong thing from my point of view.'

Dorcas thought it strange that she was being allowed to talk so freely and at such length without even an interruptive duck of sympathetic understanding or a dry cough to indicate that her listener was bored silly. When she did look up, peeping a glance from beneath cautiously lifting lids, she saw why. The poor exhausted soul was fast asleep. Her white hair lay sparsely on the pillow, in sleep her fragile features had recaptured the vulnerability they had known as a child. And, childlike, one hand lay crumpled under her cheek.

With an outsize lump in her throat, Dorcas smoothed the top sheet, tensed to kiss a pale cheek, and tiptoed quietly out of the room.

At about this point, Dorcas admitted to herself that the old señora had not deliberately set out to trap a confidence from her. Rather,

Dorcas had selected Carlos's grandmother as confidante, because the compulsion to tell someone had been so great that it would not stand bottling up a moment longer. She'd had to invest the role of inquisitor upon someone, and Carlos's grandmother had admirably fitted this part. Thinking about it now, it seemed very weak-minded of her. But no harm done. She felt better for having got it out of her system, and she didn't mind—and even admitted to being relieved—that the old señora had fallen asleep.

*　　　*　　　*

Doña Madelena stayed for five days. Dorcas was overjoyed to be appointed chauffeuse. Rose Ruiz broached the idea at breakfast that first morning.

'Dorcas, not so long ago you came to me and told me the inactivity of having nothing to do was getting on your nerves. You asked me if there was anything you could do. Well, there is. No, don't give your consent until you've heard me out, because what I have in mind might not appeal. And before I say anything, I must check a few facts. I am right, aren't I, in thinking you are qualified to drive?'

'Yes. In the latter years, when grandmother couldn't get around very well, she bought an old car. I took a course of driving lessons, went in for and passed my test, and drove her

174

wherever she wanted to go.'

'It seems you are better qualified for the job I have in mind for you than I first thought. But what about in this country? Are you permitted to drive here? Look, I'll explain. My mother-in-law has friends in the district whom she likes to call on while she is staying with us. The usual thing is to put a car at her disposal and someone to drive it for her. I can't drive. I never made the effort to learn when I was young and I'm too set in my ways, and too much of a coward, to try now. So it's usual to appoint a member of the staff to drive her around. It's always a bit of a headache finding someone with sufficient tact and stamina. I hardly need to go into that . . . you know what she is. Anyway, as you seem to get on so well with her, I thought it might seem friendlier if you drove her about. So what do you say? If you haven't got the necessary cover to drive here, I suppose it could easily be arranged.'

'No problem there. I made provision to drive in Spain before I came. I rented a car at first. I suppose I never mentioned this before because the subject never cropped up. I quite like driving. And it's true that I seem to get on well with doña Madelena. So . . .'

'You mean you'll do it? Brave girl, not to be intimidated by my mother-in-law.'

'I wouldn't go as far as to say that. But even taking all my qualms into consideration, I think I shall quite enjoy it.'

And Dorcas did enjoy it. She remembered how it had been when she drove her grandmother to see her friends. No matter how tranquilly she sat, they didn't want a young girl listening to their reminiscences, and so her grandmother had insisted on Dorcas dropping her off and calling back later to collect her.

Dorcas mentioned this to doña Madelena, and asked if this method might also suit her. The señora's bright eyes searched Dorcas's face thoroughly as though looking for some flaw. She shook her head on some private thought of her own, but still made no attempt to speak.

Finding such scrutiny uncomfortable, Dorcas asked: 'Have I a smut on my nose or something?'

'You are without blemish. This is what my eyes tell me. Then I remind myself that the eyes are simply windows that let in images for the brain to interpret. My brain comes up with the same message. You are a truly remarkable girl. Very kind, very thoughtful of what is best for others. It is wrong of me to question such a selfless outlook—it is a rare and beautiful thing to meet such unselfishness in these modern times—but I am going to say this to you, child. Just occasionally, give a thought to what is best for you.'

The praise brought a blush to her cheeks and a deprecating croak to her throat.

Doña Madelena continued: 'It is true that my friends and I prefer to be left to ourselves while we wallow in memories. If you were present, they would feel the need to entertain you. But if you leave me as you suggest and call back to collect me later, how will you fill in the time?'

'With so much to see of your beautiful countryside, señora, how can you ask that?'

'A most predictable reply. We will strike a compromise. You will deposit me, but you will return half an hour before I am ready to leave, so that my friends can share the delight of knowing you.'

This arrangement, which had much to commend itself to all parties, worked well. It enabled Dorcas to see more of the surrounding district. Sometimes she abandoned the car by the roadside and walked, skirting round olive groves and orchards, and if she trespassed nobody seemed to mind. Other times she absorbed herself by looking in the local shops. She still had a limited amount of her holiday money left, and she looked with an eye to buying suitable thank-you presents for her host and hostess. So far she hadn't seen anything special enough. She saw, and bought, a casket of English chocolates, which would later do duty as a needlework box, and which she knew would appeal to doña Madelena. The señora had a passion for the dark English chocolate that was not as sweet as the Continental variety. A taste that her English daughter-in-law had very probably introduced her to. Then, shop or countryside browsing done, she would call at the particular friend's house doña Madelena was visiting and enjoy the resultant fuss that was made of her. It was not one-sided; the ladies of doña Madelena's acquaintance took equal delight in meeting Dorcas, finding pleasant diversion in a new— and so happy—face.

Dorcas couldn't ever remember feeling this happy before. She was so happy, she was afraid. Because she felt that nobody was allowed to be this happy. All the worries, the prickles and irritations, had gone to ground. Michael still went out most evenings, a pointer that he was seeing someone, but did it have to be Isabel Roca? Don Enrique, despite the occasion of that talk in his study when putting her in the picture seemed to be putting her out of Carlos's life, had never stopped being her kind señor; his manner was as benign as ever towards her. Her relationship with Rose Ruiz was without strain and had found its own friendly level. And—best of all—Carlos telephoned her every evening.

The separation had not hindered the progress of love, but had given it a new sweetness and impetus. Carlos said intimate and loving things to her that stung her cheeks a lively pink. He called her his own precious

178

love, and told her how empty his heart had been until she came to fill it. He said that when he returned he would give her no respite, he would plague her by day and haunt her dreams by night, until she gave him the reply he wanted to hear.

The distance between them made her bold and spiced her replies with coquetry. 'I cannot think what this question can be, no matter how hard I put my mind to it.'

'That is where you make your mistake. It is no use looking to the mind. You must search your heart.'

Dorcas smiled cryptically on the thought that her heart wouldn't hold still long enough for a lengthy probe. Its erratic beat told her it was time to take a graceful step backwards from the easy intimacy they had fallen into. To proceed, to allot it greater importance than a moment of fun, was the way to folly and heartache. Fun? She had always credited herself with an elastic imagination. Her imagination's notion of fun would not stretch to cover this situation. She felt as though she was poised on a high thin wire. She could neither move forward nor backwards, nor keep her balance. Her perspective had gone haywire. She had only a fingertip hold on self-preservation.

'Won't it create too many problems, Carlos?' she asked, trying to sound normally conversational, but failing to keep the catch of excitement out of her voice.

'Problems, yes. But with the substance of mist, and beyond . . . sunshine.'

Her hope, his belief, melted over her features. She could no more evict the smile from her lips than she could stop herself falling under the spell of charm and cajolery Carlos dispensed without effort. Her will to remain cool and untouched sank to meet the upsurge of tears she savagely blinked from her eyes as she spoke the explicit fear. 'Your memory is playing you false. Your mind has painted a picture of me that I cannot live up to. When you return and see me as I am, you will not want to ask your question.'

'I could not be so ungallant. Having dishonoured you . . .'

'I'm sorry. I didn't quite catch that.'

'In thought.'

'In thought?'

'You were with me all last night.'

'Oh, Carlos.'

'Where were your thoughts?'

'With you,' she said in a voice that barely rose above a whisper.

'What did I tell you? You are compromised. Have you no shame? You admit to spending the night with me . . .'

'Only in thought, Carlos,' she butted in urgently.

'There you go again. Arguing with me, instead of being grateful that I am offering to

180

make an honest woman of you.'

It was a deliciously absurd, delightfully wicked conversation that could never have taken place with eye to eye contact.

'I am grateful, Carlos,' she said demurely. She was grateful for his . . . He hadn't come out in the open and said he loved her yet. He had not said 'I love you' in those precise words, but surely that's what he meant. So . . . grateful for his love.

'Nothing else?' he said.

'Of course something else,' she replied with shy reserve.

His laugh was throaty. 'It's all right. I won't make you own to it first.'

Own to what? Love?

'*Buenas noches, querida.* I'll hold you in my dreams.'

And I'll hold you in mine, she thought, shivering on the implication. But all she said was a sedate: '*Buenas noches*, Carlos.'

She put down the telephone receiver and turned to see Michael pretending to look detached, while selecting a carnation from the vase on the hall table for his buttonhole. He looked across at her. His face was painfully easy to read. She had lived with Michael long enough to know she was in for a bout of unkind teasing.

'Carlos beginning to show his gratitude, eh?'

She thought back to her telephone conversation with Carlos. Gratitude had been mentioned, but her gratitude not his. Had Michael latched on to the wrong meaning? No, she thought, spotting the calculated gleam in his eye.

Her inside seemed to sink away from her into a vast emptiness. Although had never truly believed that Michael could alter, she had hoped he might.

'I don't know what you mean,' she said levelly.

This man was her brother, yet she felt as far removed from him as any star in the universe.

'Don't you?' he taunted. Adding obscurely: 'It's all right, Dorcas. I won't take your pride from you. You need it.'

What did he mean? What made him say she needed her pride? She felt as awkward and as exposed as if he had indeed taken it; she didn't know the words to say to get it back. She didn't say anything.

'I suppose gratitude is as good a basis as any, and sufficient for a woman's needs.'

His bland smile jarred even more than his sneering tone. Dorcas found herself wanting to clutch her arms to suppress the shivers.

'You are insulting me. Please tell me why.'

For several seconds they found common interest in just looking at one another. Michael did a surprising about-turn and became very contrite.

'I have fairly recently been told that I am not a very nice person, so could that be a

182

possible reason?'

Being told this home-truth—by whom?—had obviously shaken him. His cool and poise were less evident, and for an incredible moment he looked as vulnerable as Dorcas felt. 'Who told you that?'

'Does it matter?'

'I think it does,' Dorcas said perceptively, 'to you. You know, Michael, if you used your golden little-boy charm for good instead of the other, you could be quite an engaging asset to have around.'

'Being good is such a taxing exercise,' he drawled.

'You don't have to be all good. I'm not suggesting you discard your horns for a pair of wings. Couldn't you be middle of the road?'

'I very much doubt it. I've always excelled in everything I've done.'

'That's true,' she said, heaving up a big sigh.

'Don't sigh for me, little sister. It will all come right.'

'I'm quite sure of that. You'll make it come right.'

'I'm not sure I like that, but I'll forgive you.'

'Forgive me?' she gasped, feeling once again that the situation had been twisted round on her.

Two blinks later, his step as jaunty as ever, Michael was marching down the hall away from her. It occurred to her that she was letting the opportunity to nail him about his activities calmly walk away. She caught up with him at the door. But before she questioned him about his affairs, she wanted to know what he meant when he said she needed her pride, and what else had he said? Something about gratitude being as good a basis as any.

'Not so fast, Michael. What's this about the gratitude bit?'

'I shouldn't have said that. I was hitting back. My plans have received an unexpected set-back. I didn't see why yours should be all smooth-running.'

'But you did say it. And having said it, you must explain.'

'It's unpleasant medicine.'

'Something for my own good, you mean, that will leave an unpalatable taste in my mouth?'

'Very explicitly put.'

'You're not just leaving it there.'

'I am. If you want to know more, you must ask Carlos.'

'Ask Carlos? But . . . ?'

While she was stupefying on that thought, Michael made his escape. Dorcas still hadn't extracted from him the name of the person he was going to meet.

* * *

The next day was doña Madelena's last full day. Contemplating the thought over a breakfast-time cup of tea, Dorcas wondered how she would cope with the inactivity once the señora had returned to her own home. A demanding and sometimes querulous-tongued matriarch she might be, but Dorcas had grown fond of her and would miss being at her beck and call. The thought of having sixty minutes in every hour to call her own rested dully on her brain. Perhaps she would pay Tom Bennett's fiancée a visit. She had spotted the English girl—no prizes for guessing this was Tom's fiancée—on at least two occasions while passing through the small Spanish town. Each time she had been chauffeuring the señora to one of her friend's houses. Had she been alone she would have stopped and introduced herself.

But she would think about how she was going to fill in her time tomorrow. No time now to waste on pensive thoughts. She was going to enjoy today to its last precious moment.

The programme was hectic. So many dear friends to be visited for a last farewell, with innumerable stops on the way for old, but still sparkling eyes to soak up a memory of a favourite view. The shadows that crept over the earth as night fell were repeated as shadows of tiredness beneath those same eyes, their lustre impaired by the demands of a day which would have jaded a much younger person.

They returned to the villa with scarcely time to change for dinner. Dorcas stepped under the shower, dropping with fatigue. The stinging missile points of water revived her. She dressed quickly, selecting a favourite dress of deep aquamarine that complemented both her tan and her figure. There was insufficient time to shampoo her hair, so she attacked it with long, crackling strokes, brushing out the dust of the day until the curling tips blazed gold.

She was ready and there was still time to take the señora the casket of chocolates she had bought as a farewell gift. Dorcas was glad of the excuse to slip along to the señora's room. She wanted to check that doña Madelena hadn't overtired herself. It was a bit late to think about it now, but it had been irresponsible of her to allow an old lady of eighty-plus to hare about like an eighteen year old. She should have insisted—no, much too emphatic—so gently and discreetly introduced a slower pace.

What Dorcas expected to find she did not quite know. It was a relief to see the tiny figure dressed and putting the final touches to her toilette. In basic black, her silver hair shining through a lace mantilla that dipped to a peak on her forehead, she was perfect in every detail. A serenely beautiful face, a frail little body, a backbone of steel. The sheer physical impact of her took Dorcas's breath away.

Dorcas advanced, sweetly hesitant, paying homage with her eyes as she offered her gift. 'It isn't much. I didn't know what to get you.' She felt awkward, but looked as appealing as a child.

'How very sweet of you, *niña*.' And the señora produced a jeweller's box. 'I have a little something for you. I hope you like my gift as much as I like yours.'

The box was long and thin in shape. Dorcas opened it up and took out a choker-length necklace. She spent several moments exclaiming how beautiful it was. When she realized it was not a pretty costume piece, but that the fragile links of chain were gold, she spent several moments protesting that it was far too expensive for her to accept.

Fixing Dorcas with an innocent look, doña Madelena said: 'Suddenly I cannot understand a word you say. Yet only a short while ago I was thinking how well you were coping with our language. It is very strange.'

'Very strange indeed,' said Dorcas. Oh well . . . . nothing else for it. 'Thank you very much for the necklace, señora.'

'Now that is much better. I understood every word. I am so pleased you have regained your fluency. Your arm, Dorcas,' she said imperiously.

Enrique Ruiz elected to drive his mother home the next day. It was Rose Ruiz who suggested: 'Perhaps Dorcas would like to go with you for the ride?'

Dorcas's mouth gave a quick lift of delight.

Enrique Ruiz pulled at his beard. 'An excellent idea. I would have mentioned it myself had I thought of it. I take it from your smile that you agree, Dorcas?'

'Oh yes! I'll go and get ready. I won't be long. I promise not to keep you waiting.'

Rose Ruiz walked with them to the car to wave them off. Kisses were exchanged between mother and daughter-in-law; goodbyes said.

Rose Ruiz turned to her husband. 'It might amuse you to let Dorcas have a turn at driving.'

'Now you know it would not,' he chided gently. 'I never allow a woman to drive me.'

'Well perhaps you . . .' She changed her mind, swallowed whatever misgivings were bothering her, and said: '*Adiós.*'

Her wave was utterly carefree and Dorcas thought she must have imagined that a shadow of unease had ever crossed her smiling face. Rose Ruiz's concern could only have been about her husband's health. Yet he looked in excellent form. His face was without strain. In casting off his dark business suit in favour of casual sweater and slacks, he had also cast off several years. Dorcas settled back to enjoy the journey.

They passed through farming country. Enrique Ruiz kept up an interesting commentary. 'The sickle and the wooden

188

plough have given way to the combine and tractor, but the water is still lifted from wells dug a thousand years ago by the Arabs. Observe the many trees. The tree is the farmer's friend. It takes from the soil and it gives back its leaves which rot and enrich the ground below.'

The road began to climb. A thin haze danced over the soaring mountain tops. Dorcas darted fascinated looks down at the sea. Flights of stone steps, lined with trees, led up to villas. But no house looked down on doña Madelena's.

Doña Madelena insisted on their staying for an unhurried lunch. It was five o'clock before they left. The last time Dorcas had experienced the perilous road down, Carlos had been at the wheel. In places the road skimmed dangerously close to the cliff edge and its sheer drop to the sea. She had forgotten how barbarous and beautiful this stretch of coast was, and how frightening. Except that she hadn't been frightened that other time. She had felt perfectly safe and relaxed in Carlos's competent care. Yet don Enrique was no less proficient a driver. He eased the car round the bends with a caution that Carlos would have scorned. Carlos still leapt at life with the arrogance and impatience of youth. Don Enrique, with the wisdom of years behind him, acknowledged that man was not invincible; old age was not achieved by chance. Dorcas should have felt safer with don Enrique. It was Rose Ruiz, with her funny unsaid fear that had put her on edge.

The town was reached without mishap. Dorcas relaxed. It happened swiftly and without warning. The child dashed out of an alleyway and ran straight into the path of the car. Don Enrique swerved to miss the child and slammed on the brake. The scream of the tyres mingled with the scream in Dorcas's throat.

She pulled at the door handle, fell out of the car and hurried across to the child, a boy with huge shocked eyes and a pulled-down mouth which opened on a protesting yell as he began to cry in earnest.

'You didn't hit him. Thanks to that really superb piece of driving.'

It was the English girl Dorcas had seen about the town who had spoken.

Dorcas opened her mouth to reply, but something—relief?—had closed her throat.

She swallowed the lump down. 'I . . . I . . .' Her eyes flashed back to the car where Enrique Ruiz was curled over the steering wheel. Dear God, no!

'See to him,' said the English girl. 'I'll stay with the boy.'

'Yes . . . yes of course.' With the flat of her hands she pushed herself up off the ground where she had been crouching, and ran back to the car.

'Señor . . .? Don Enrique?' she said, using the respectful but friendly form of address for the first time.

The crumpled shoulders lifted. 'I am all right, *niña*. Go back to the *muchacho.*'

Dorcas stared into the shock-frozen features. 'You didn't hit him. He's shaken up, that's all. I've said I'll come back. Right now I'm going to drive you home. Move over.'

'I will not permit a woman to drive me. I am perfectly capable. But,' with a slight, concessionary smile, 'if it will please you, I will allow you to sit with me. Then, if you are certain you feel up to it, you may have the car to drive back and ensure that the boy has taken no harm. Find out his name and address. Inform the boy's mama that I will call on her within a day or so to compensate him for his fright and satisfy myself all is well. Will you do this for me?'

Dorcas said she would, and settled herself in the passenger seat. What else could she do?

At the villa, she left it to don Enrique to explain to his wife, slid behind the wheel, turned the car round and drove back to town. A small ring of spectators marked the spot.

Tom's fiancée was in charge of the situation. She had calmed the boy down. Her arm was round his shoulders and his skinny body was pressed close into her side. She was holding him not as a troublesome nuisance, but as a precious individual who had honoured her by

191

accepting the comfort she was only too pleased to give. The warmth in her eyes, the trust in his, was really something.

'I've promised to buy Pepe the biggest ham sandwich he's ever seen. As soon as the shock has subsided and I'm reasonably confident he won't be sick.'

'Have you found out where he lives?'

'Off the main square. But it's no good taking him home yet because his mama works in that vegetable and flower shop next to the fish market.' Giving the thin shoulders a squeeze, she said: 'Isn't he a pet. You don't suppose his mama will let me keep him?'

'No. You'll have to get one of your own.'

'I'll order one by mail catalogue.' Her bitter laugh and cynical tone embarrassed Dorcas. 'Silly me! It's the other male it involves.'

'That shouldn't present a difficulty,' Dorcas said, puzzled.

'That's what I thought too,' she said, looking pointedly down at her engagement ring.

Dorcas continued to look awkward and miserable. If things weren't working out for Tom Bennett and his fiancée, she was the last person to want to probe.

She was greatly relieved when Tom's fiancée smiled breezily and said: 'Come on. Let's buy Pepe that sandwich. By the time he's eaten it his mama should be home.'

When Dorcas got back to the villa, Rose

192

Ruiz told her that her husband was resting in his room.

'I'm afraid he can't stand shocks like this. I'm glad you were on hand, Dorcas. Did you get the details he asked for?'

'It's all written down here. The name of the boy and the names of his parents and their address. I've even jotted down where his parents work. Try not to worry, señora.'

'The boy? Is he unharmed?'

'Yes. You know what boys are. He's already looking upon it as an adventure, and enjoying the fuss being made of him.'

'That is good. You have done well, my dear.' Her crisp, matter-of-fact tone was skimpy cover for her concern. 'I'm so glad Enrique didn't hurt the boy. It would have . . .' She didn't finish.

At the foot of the stairs she turned to face Dorcas. 'I almost forgot. Carlos phoned while you were out. He was sorry to miss you. Your brother is in the *sala*. Why don't you ask him to pour you a drink? You've earned it.'

'I'll do that,' said Dorcas, thinking a drink wasn't much of a sop for missing Carlos's phone call.

She joined her brother who wanted to know what she and the señor had been up to. She told him. Not wanting to dwell on the matter, she abruptly changed the subject.

'Michael?'

'Yes?'

Though of the same colour, there was a cloud in her eyes that was not repeated in the glass of sherry in her hand. 'Last time we talked, you made certain inferences. I got the impression that you'd been talking to Carlos about me. I want to know what was said.'

'What persistence!' Michael's handsome mouth curled up in a smile. 'I said to him, now look here, Charlie boy, what are you going to do about my sister?'

'I sincerely hope you are joking.'

'What do you think?'

'I don't know what to think. That's why I'm asking, and getting precious little sense, too.'

To her shame she knew that her temper was in danger of snapping. She took a deep breath. Said calmly and rationally: 'Try to explain it to me without the funny cracks.'

'You're making something out of nothing, Dorcas. But very well. I thought Carlos should have it straight that in saving Feli and the kid, you'd wrote finis to your dancing career.'

'I already know that much. If there's more, go on.'

'He said he was very sorry and that he wouldn't have had it happen for anything, but that dancing wasn't the only fulfilment. He said a warm person like you would find greater satisfaction in a husband and children. I asked him if he was telling me something. He gave me a long, sort of thoughtful look and said, Do you know I think I am. Well, then I gave him

194

my blessing and said that I was glad he was doing the right thing by you.'

'Oh, Michael. Oh no! You didn't! You couldn't have! You've got this fixation that I'm owed something. I hope you know what you've done. You've only made it impossible for me to accept Carlos's proposal. I can't accept a proposal that's been made at pistol point. *She* was right.'

'Who was?'

'The girl who said you weren't a very nice person.' He didn't say it wasn't a girl. He didn't say anything.

'Was it Isabel?'

'No. Isabel thinks I'm a very nice person. Don't meddle in my affairs, Dorcas,' he warned in an ominously quiet voice.

'Why not? You've meddled in mine.'

'I've only tried to help.'

The frustrating part of it was, he thought he was helping. His motive was suspect, but not his sincerity.

Michael went out as usual that evening. Dorcas was glad. She couldn't have faced him across the dining table. The meal was taken in quiet preoccupation. Don Enrique put in an appearance, but he was concerned with his own thoughts. Rose Ruiz was concerned for her husband. Her glance of quiet affection scarcely left his strained face. The household retired early that night.

Dorcas had not been asleep all that long

195

when Teresa came to wake her.

The little maid urgently jogged her arm. 'Wake up, señorita. Please, please wake up.'

Not only was Dorcas's mind dulled by sleep, but she was slowed down by her limited knowledge of the language. Teresa was speaking much too quickly for Dorcas to follow. The words themselves meant nothing, it was the quality of Teresa's despair that registered on her reasoning.

Amid the spate of Spanish she caught the word that told her someone was gravely ill. Her sleep addled brain skipped back to doña Madelena's last exhausting day.

'Oh no!' she gasped. 'I knew I was wrong to let doña Madelena put so much effort into her farewells. I've been expecting this.'

Teresa stared at her blankly. 'No, no, señorita. It is not the old señora who is . . .' This time Teresa did not say ill, she said . . . 'dying.'

No, of course not. Now Dorcas remembered that she and don Enrique had taken the señora home and left her in good health and high spirits. So who . . . ?

'The señor,' Teresa was saying. 'It is the señor.' She was weeping and twisting her hands in agitation.

Not her kind señor! And it all came back to Dorcas. The shock of nearly running over Pepe had been too great for Enrique Ruiz. She remembered seeing him crumpled over the

196

steering wheel of his car. She had been so terribly afraid that it had been too much for his heart. And obviously it had been.

She pulled back the single sheet and scrambled out of bed, his name on her lips. 'Don Enrique, I knew it. I knew the strain was too much for his heart.'

'No, no, señorita. You do not understand. It is not *el señor jefe*. It is the young señor.'

Dorcas's heart tripped painfully on its beat. Carlos! His name whispered like a chill wind across her bitterly frozen brain.

Teresa was saying: 'I wonder you did not hear the noise as they carried him to his room. There is so much blood. Blood everywhere. *El jefe* is on the phone to *el señor doctor*. The señora told me to come and tell you.'

'Was it a driving accident? Carlos goes much, much too fast in his car. For pity's sake, don't keep me in suspense like this. Tell me, Teresa.'

Her words leapt into the air; died. Her mind was swept clean of all but the one fact. Carlos was hurt. It didn't matter now. He was hurt and he was here in this house, and she was wasting valuable time.

CHAPTER NINE

Teresa caught her by the strap of her cotton nightgown before she reached the bedroom door. She held out a dressing gown to her, as if the proprieties had to be observed even at a time like this.

Teresa said so gravely and so sadly: 'It is not *el* señor Carlos *de* Ruiz.'

'No?'

Dorcas's spirits lifted, soared like a bird. Someone was hurt and later she would sorrow about that, but at this precious moment she could only rejoice because it wasn't Carlos.

'It is your brother, señorita. Señor West.'

'Michael?'

Remorse came quickly. It was all Dorcas could do to prevent her teeth from chattering. Making a huge effort, she thanked Teresa for the dressing gown, and fastened herself into it as she went.

Michael's bedroom seemed to be full of people. Her eyes flew beyond them to the still figure on the bed.

'What happened? Was it a car accident?'

Don Enrique had put a car at Michael's disposal. She was obsessed with the thought that it had to be a car accident. Yet if Michael had been pulled out of a wrecked car, surely, in the condition he was in, he would have been taken straight to hospital? Teresa was right about the blood. It was everywhere. His hair was matted with it; it was on his face and his neck and richly spattered on his white shirt front.

She felt sick. A pair of hands reached out for her. One went round her shoulders. The other took and lifted her chin and she found herself looking into Carlos's gravely concerned eyes.

She said idiotically: 'How could you get here so quickly?'

'I couldn't. I completed my business a day earlier than anticipated. I had intended staying the one more night and travelling home in the morning when I was fresh. On an impulse, or a whim, I booked out tonight. I've only just got here.'

'So it could have been you involved in the car crash.'

'What car crash?'

His eyes reflected her bewilderment.

'The one Michael was involved in. Teresa told me the young señor was hurt, and I thought it was you.'

'Hurt, yes. Not in a car crash, but in a fight.'

Around about this time, Dorcas began to identify other people in the room. Enrique Ruiz and, of course, Rose, his wife. Two—no three members of the staff, and surprisingly the Spaniard Dorcas had met at Tom Bennett's garage, Paco Garcia, whom she remembered was Alfonso Roca's right-hand man.

The compulsion of her gaze made Paco Garcia look up. He was as surprised to see Dorcas as she was to see him. Dorcas brought her attention back to Carlos.

'Who was Michael fighting? Why was he fighting?'

Carlos chose to answer the second question first. 'It was over a woman. Isn't it always? It was never meant to reach this stage. I can personally vouch that Michael's opponent is not a violent man. But, things were said, tempers flared out of control. The mallet was there and . . .'

'Mallet? What mallet?'

'A chef's mallet. The argument took place in a restaurant. The speciality dish of this restaurant is chicken with a rich seasoning, topped with foie gras and truffles. It is brought to the table in a sealed clay pot. With it comes a mallet to crack open the pot. The mallet can be quite a vicious weapon when brought down on a man's head with force.'

'Which is what happened to Michael. I know my brother can be the most infuriating person at times, but who would want to—who *did* such a thing?'

'Paco Garcia. We don't know Michael's side of it yet, but knowing Paco as I do, the provocation must have been justified. It looks bad, I know. It's true that Michael has lost a lot of blood, but he has youth and a healthy constitution on his side. He was in the peak of physical fitness when this happened, and that must stand him in good stead.'

Dorcas knew she should be grateful for the platitudes. Instead of having the desired calming effect, they irritated her. She wanted fact, however gruesome, not supposition, however comforting.

Fact: The doctor had been sent for. Where was he? Head injuries are always serious. The doctor should be here now. Fact: Michael and Paco Garcia had been fighting over a woman. What was her name?

'I want you to look after Isabel,' Carlos said. 'Will you do this for me while I try to find out what is keeping the doctor?'

'Isabel! Is she here?' Dorcas said in surprise.

Her glance stretched round the room to where Isabel was sitting. She wore a glowing ruby gown with an insert of black lace following the swell of her breasts. Her black lace mantilla was supported by a high tortoiseshell comb. Dimly at the back of Dorcas's mind was the thought that the mantilla, worn in this way with a high comb, was reserved for special occasions. Nothing enhances a woman's beauty more than to have her face framed in black lace, with a black lace peak teasing down on her forehead. But what struck Dorcas more than Isabel's beauty was her bird-like fragility. Her raven-black eyes pecked out troubled looks in her pale, trapped face. She thinks Michael is going to die, thought Dorcas.

Dorcas bit her lip hard and turned savagely on Carlos. 'Why wasn't Michael taken to hospital? If he'd been taken straight to hospital, he would have had instant medical attention.'

'I agree. Don't blame me. I wasn't there, remember?'

'No. Michael was there, and Paco Garcia was there. Presumably the woman they were fighting over was there?'

The question invited more than Carlos's brief: 'Yes.' He added: 'The details will have to wait. I'm wasting time. I must find out what is happening.'

The hand on her shoulder dropped to give her fingers a brief squeeze. Before he left the room, he paused to have a word with Isabel Roca. The Spanish girl immediately got up and came over to sit next to Dorcas.

'Carlos has gone to hurry things up.'

'Yes.'

Dorcas wondered where Isabel fitted in all this. She had already decided in her mind that Michael had made trouble between Paco and his woman. Had Isabel also been dining at the restaurant? If she had been there to see what happened, it would explain her being here. She looked, somehow, too young to be caught up

202

in this unsavoury situation.

'How old are you Isabel?' Dorcas asked unexpectedly.

'That is an odd question,' said Isabel. 'I have eighteen years.'

'You're only a child.'

'I wish I were. Two grown men wouldn't fight over a child.'

'Good heavens!' Dorcas said slowly.

'You mean you didn't know?'

'Silly of me, but no. Isn't that ridiculous? I should have known. I'm sure I would have got round to it eventually. Carlos said Michael and Señor Garcia were fighting over a woman. I assumed it was Señor Garcia's woman.'

'You assumed right.' Two bright blobs of colour invaded Isabel's cheeks. She put her fingers up, as if to rub the colour out, and said with touching dignity and just a feather stirring of wistfulness: 'It was never Carlos. I never pretended to you that it was. It has been Paco for as long as I can remember. Paco is a valued employee of Papa's. Yet Papa would never acknowledge Paco as a husband for me. Paco knew that Carlos must have first claim.'

'Did you resent this?'

'I don't know what you mean.'

'I'm not quite sure I know myself. But . . . because you knew that Paco would never fight with Carlos for you, did you purposely provoke him by flirting with Michael?'

'That is not a kind thing to say.'

Dorcas could have said, this is not a kind thing to have happened to Michael. But she said: 'You are quite right, Isabel. I spoke without thinking. I'm not blaming you for what happened.' Her words said one thing; the lack of conviction in her tone, another.

Isabel gave a small tormented sigh. 'Your brother is gravely ill. Of course you want to kick at me. But it is not true that I deliberately set out to flirt with him. At first, perhaps, a little . . . but then I fight to resist his advances. This I find difficult, because I have the powerful fascination for him. You see this?'

'Only too well. My brother is a fascinating person.'

Dorcas remembered how thin the dividing line was between love and fascination. If Isabel could name the emotion she felt for Michael as infatuation and not love, she had achieved something that perplexed older and more worldly women.

A hand touched Dorcas's. She lifted her eyes to see Carlos looking down at her.

'The doctor is here. I must ask everyone to leave the room while he makes his examination.'

'Of course,' said Dorcas, getting quickly to her feet.

The sad little party huddled in groups in the *sala*. Instinctively, Dorcas and Isabel moved out to the terrace for privacy. The chilly night air had a bracing, invigorating effect.

204

The compulsion in Isabel was to talk. Dorcas let her.

'At first when Michael asks me to go out with him for the evening, I say no. But he keeps asking, and I am weak. I think, what harm can it do? And then, it is as if I have not the mind to think with. I am bewitched. I hide my feelings from Mama and Papa, but not from Paco. Many times Paco tries to reason with me. He says I am hurting myself. That hardly seems to matter. What does matter, what troubles me is that I am hurting Paco. It has long been Papa's wish that I marry Carlos. This Paco understands. What he cannot understand—and I cannot explain it to myself, never mind to him—is this wildness that has entered my blood for Michael. I have not realized until this moment the selflessness of Paco's love for me. He wants only what is best for me. And I have brought this dreadful trouble on him.'

She paused to swallow. Her eyes were full of pain, and Dorcas thought, if she grips her hands any harder the bones will break.

'It is most unfortunate that Paco should also choose to dine at *Las Palmeras* this evening. Michael said he wished to sample the famous *pollo*, the chicken, which is brought to the table in a sealed clay pot. Michael made fun of the sarcophagus-like shape of the pot. The ritual of serving this speciality dish is taken very seriously. Michael had been drinking heavily. He wasn't in the mood to take anything seriously. He made jokes that were in bad taste. I tried to shut him up, but it was impossible. In my foolishness I was glad when Paco intervened. Perhaps I asked him to. Oh, not in so many words, but I think perhaps my eyes signalled a message to where he was sitting a few tables away. He threw down his napkin and came striding over to our table. He was very angry, but in a controlled sort of way. I was so proud of him. He politely asked Michael to conduct himself in a more seemly manner. He said Michael should consider the dignity of my position. Michael laughed in his face. He said terrible things to Paco. Things no man of honour could accept. He insulted his manhood. It was horrible . . . horrible. Paco was goaded into doing what he did. He picked up the mallet and brought it down on Michael's head, but his is the least guilt. Michael and I are the guilty ones. So you see, don't you, that I could not let Paco take the blame?'

'Yes. But I don't see how you could prevent it.'

'When the manager said he was going to telephone the *policia*, I asked him not to. I asked him what all the fuss was about. I said that Michael had lost his balance while getting to his feet and had struck his head on the edge of the table, which was hardly a matter for the police. The manager, poor man, looked quite relieved. Not unnaturally he didn't want the *guardia* poking around. It would give the place a bad name. Although what Michael will say when . . .'

If he comes round, thought Dorcas. Aloud she said: 'He will say you did right.' Her voice sounded dry even to herself. 'My brother has never been too keen on police intervention.'

The hands that had been so tightly gripping each other, reached out and took Dorcas's. Instant tears came to Isabel's eyes. 'How very generous of you. What can I say but thank you.' Her gratitude that Dorcas understood was heartfelt and flowed from her, as unimpeded as the tears now coursing freely down her cheeks. 'I expected to be scolded for trying to protect Paco. And instead . . .'

'Instead I am going to scold you for thinking I would react differently. I love my brother dearly, but I am not blinded to his faults. I can well believe that Paco acted under stress and provocation.' Had Michael taunted Paco for standing meekly to one side while Carlos took his girl? Had he accused him of not being a man? It was not difficult to imagine the sort of thing Michael had said. Dorcas sighed. 'You are right in saying the guilt is not his, but I think you might have a hard time convincing him. You must go to Paco at once. He needs your support and comfort.'

'Yes . . . yes. I must go to Paco. And not just for the moment, either. I've been such an idiot in thinking I could make a life with someone else. How would it please Papa to see me unhappy? Papa who loves me and wants only my happiness will have to see that Paco is the only man for me. Do you realize what this means, Dorcas? It means that Carlos will be free to court you.'

'I have just this second digested that fact. I hope you don't think I said what I did to suit my own purpose?'

'Of course not! Who's being an idiot now? Oh, Dorcas, I'm so ashamed. I should feel miserable. Instead I feel happy.'

'You're being an idiot now, that's who. There's nothing to feel miserable about. Michael is going to get better.'

'You're an angel. Please, please be right about Michael. I hope things go well with you and Carlos.'

Isabel's long skirt brushed against Dorcas's ankle. She hastened inside to find Paco, drying her tears as she went.

Dorcas sat on for only a hand-count of seconds before she too went inside. In the *sala*, she saw that Isabel had gone to Paco. Even as Dorcas watched, Isabel's fingers wound themselves round his. Paco's startled reaction was reflected in his eyes. He knew Isabel was making a declaration; he seemed uncertain whether to let her. At least, that's how it seemed to Dorcas. Towering above the two sitting figures—as if he had just that moment risen to give Isabel his seat—Carlos wore a troubled look. His quick intelligence would have summed up the situation. With dropping dismay, Dorcas saw how his expression searched down into a frown.

Oh, Carlos, *no!* Oh, my love. Not *you!* Sometimes it happens that way. Feelings are discovered too late. The realization that you love someone coming when the loved-one is lost to you. But it didn't happen to well-integrated people like Carlos. The fact that she would have staked her reputation on Carlos's clear-sighted judgement made it all the harder to bear.

It was the dangling carrot that was so edibly and sweetly within reach. Her teeth had scraped its surface; this time it had seemed impossible for happiness to be denied her but, just like all the other times, at the very last moment was it to be snatched away from her? And yet, those other disappointments were but trivial pin-pricks in comparison with her disappointment now.

She hadn't realized she was parading her misery for everyone to see, until a kindly voice said: 'Come sit by me, dear.'

Following the direction of the voice, Dorcas found herself looking into Rose Ruiz's concerned eyes. Her fingers were taken, tightly held.

'Your hand is just like a peg of ice. That will be the shock.'

Yes, it was the shock. Although why it should come as so much of a shock she didn't know. Even the most clear-sighted person has the odd blind spot. And, goodness, hadn't she wondered often enough how Carlos could look at someone as incredibly lovely as Isabel and be indifferent to her!

'Your devotion does you credit, child, but you must not allow yourself to give way to grief. You must be strong.'

'I did not know I was so transparent. I promise to do better. I have no intention of giving way.' To prove it, Dorcas put on a brave smile.

'Good girl. That smile will be Michael's best recovery aid.'

That shock! Nothing should have taken precedence over concern for Michael's grave condition. It seemed especially shameful that her mind had been so selfishly occupied.

Totally mistaking her stricken look, Rose Ruiz piled on the approbation. 'Michael is very lucky. I can hardly think he is deserving of such a caring sister.'

Dorcas firmly contained her shame behind sealed lips. It wasn't that she didn't want to tell—just the opposite. Confession would have absolved a tiny portion of her guilt. There wasn't time to tell. Not with Carlos bearing down on them.

'Isabel's parents will be wondering where she is,' Carlos said, demonstrating his usual

210

thought for others.

A frown crossed Rose Ruiz's brow. 'You are so practical, Carlos. That thought never occurred to me. I'll telephone straight away to let them know what has happened.'

'Have you forgotten it is not possible to dial direct? The switchboard operator listens in. It would be served up in every home with the breakfast rolls.'

'M'm. You are so right. So—I'll send word with one of the servants. Now, who has the most tactful tongue? I don't want a garbled version passed on that might cause alarm.'

'The only tongue I can guarantee is my own. I'll go.'

'No, Carlos, I won't allow it. You've already had that long drive home. I don't know why you didn't wait until morning. Providence must have guided your choice, because I don't know what we would have done without you. You've been a tower of strength, but you can't be expected to do more. You look worn out.'

Rose Ruiz was right. Whether or not Carlos had been successful in his quest to stabilize the family business, the effort he'd put in had taken its toll. There was a stark, staring blankness about his eyes. He looked like a man who has not slept for a week, or a man in deep shock.

'You fuss too much,' was all he said.

Impulsively, Dorcas said: 'Let me go with you.'

211

Rose Ruiz backed up this suggestion. 'Yes, if you insist on going, then at least take Dorcas with you.'

With a slow, robot-like movement, his head turned round to Dorcas. How cold his eyes were. Coldly condemning. This puzzled her. Cold indifference she could have understood from a man so recently jolted into a change of heart. Guilt, even, because he had led her on a bit. His guilt, not hers. Yet his eyes accused her.

She fully expected him to reject her offer to accompany him. Yet it was the flavour of his acceptance that surprised her even more than the acceptance itself.

'Why not? No fear of my falling asleep over the wheel. With you by my side I'll need to keep alert.' The scorn in his voice was unbelievable. 'Don't you want to wait to hear what the doctor has to say about Michael?'

Was it concern or sarcasm that motivated this question? Dorcas was too baffled by Carlos's change of manner to tell.

'I can't alter the doctor's verdict. It will wait until I get back.'

She got to her feet. The contact of her dressing gown against her ankles reminded her that she must first go upstairs to dress. Carlos guided her to the foot of the stairs without speaking.

On the first stair she turned her head and their eyes met. He hadn't expected her to look

212

back and his unguarded expression was hurt and questioning.

'Carlos?' she said, the bright burning blood of confusion rushing to her cheeks. 'What is it? Please tell me.'

'Tell you what? That I have made a gigantic fool of myself by falling in love with a woman I thought to be quite perfect. Do you want it in gruesome detail that my love led me to believe she felt the same way, when all the time her heart was given to another. Even though everything about her, every sweet and loving look and gesture denied it, her interest in me was a pretence. Can you look me in the eye, Dorcas, and tell me truthfully this is not so.'

Dorcas dipped her head. Of course she could not. What she ought to tell him was that although Isabel had been foolish in thinking she could marry to forge a business alliance, she hadn't deliberately set out to delude him, but to please her father. An act of daughterly obedience that Carlos would surely understand.

'I'm sorry,' Dorcas said from the bottom of her heart. Sorry that Carlos had ever found out he loved Isabel. If only the discovery could have stayed hidden long enough for her to have made her mark on his affections, then perhaps he would have turned to her for warmth. If, instead of being scared silly that Carlos would think her mercenary, thanks to Michael's silly scheming and sly innuendos, she'd encouraged him . . .who knows?

The look of disgust he gave her shamed her and made her wonder if he could read her thoughts.

'It is true, then? Even when Paco told me, I hoped that by some miracle it was a lie.'

'Paco told you!'

She was surprised at Paco's forthrightness. It had been firmly fixed in her mind that he had made the observation himself by seeing them together. She thought he had identified the loving look Isabel had given Paco as an open declaration of her feelings.

The compulsion to comfort was great. Greater than her shame, greater than the risk of humiliation in rejection. Her hand reached out to touch his cheek, but it was grasped at the wrist. She felt herself being propelled none too gently forward.

'Have a care, Dorcas. We are playing a different game now, with a different set of rules to observe.'

'I don't understand. I know you've been hurt, but I don't understand why you want to hurt me.' Although his fingers cut cruelly into her wrist, it was the mental anguish she referred to. Her lashes met; she didn't want him to see the weakness of tears.

She didn't see the expression in his eyes, but she heard the bitterness and contempt in his voice. 'Michael said your hope of being a great dancer was ruined. Doesn't he know you have

214

it in you to be a greater actress than you could ever be a dancer? You are giving an Oscar performance.'

'I am not acting. I never wanted anything from you, anything material that is.'

'Ah yes! The pride your brother spoke of. He said I would have to find a more subtle way of rewarding you for the act of courage that saved Feli and Rosita at such high personal cost. He said you were an attractive, nicely constructed . . . quite so,' he said, lingering there for the time it took his eyes to leave her face and make an insulting all-over survey. ' . . . warm-hearted girl.' It was her cheeks that were warming at the manner of his inspection. 'Surely it would not be too difficult? he said. I asked him to stop hinting and come right out with it. He said that in keeping with most caring brothers, it was his wish to see his sister happily married.'

'I'll match my brother's bluntness. We both know Michael only cares about himself. It would suit him to have a rich brother-in-law. But this isn't something new to you. You've known Michael's attitude all along. It's never made you bitter before. You've even laughed about it.'

'Because his avarice highlighted your lack of it, or so I thought. You more or less said that because Michael had spoken to me of this matter, it made it impossible for you to consider it. *Cara*, you have no idea how much

215

that delighted me.' The carelessly used endearment was a knife in her heart. A piercing hurt of hope that, somehow, stitched more tightly—intensified—her dismay. 'I believed you. I thought Michael was the unethical one. Michael makes no bones about being an unscrupulous opportunist. I can at least admire him for his openness. What I cannot forgive is cupidity hiding behind the fair face of virtue. I thought you were so pure in your ideals.'

'I hope I am. I do not understand what you are talking about, but I am going to find out.'

'The game is up, Dorcas. Don't waste your acting talent on me.'

'Why are you attacking me? I haven't done anything terribly wrong, and neither has Isabel if it comes to that. You've exaggerated the issue in your mind. You've blown it up until you're not seeing straight.'

'On the contrary, I'm seeing straight for the first time.' And then on a quizzical note. 'What has Isabel to do with this?'

'Everything.'

'Forgive me for stealing your lines, but now it is I who do not understand.'

'Then please let me refresh your memory. Paco told you something. Right?'

'Yes.' The soft puzzlement went from his face and his expression tightened against her.

'What he told you put you in a flaming temper.'

'I'll concede that, too.'

'Well?'

'If that is supposed to be the conclusion of your explanation, I think you are being deliberately provocative.'

'That is the last thing I am being,' Dorcas said bitterly, untruthfully, because her restrained anger was electric provocation.

'I know what I know and I see what I see. The two are not in accord.'

His hand left her wrist to grasp the back of her neck. The fingers twisting her neck round so that he could see her face better, sent a sensuous thrill down her spine.

'What do you see, Carlos?' Her voice stole from her throat as a dry little whisper.

'I see a woman. She is desirable. I want her. She is a temptress and I am only human.' His voice was harsh with self-contempt.

He called her a temptress, but she was only human too. She stood rooted to the spot, willing him to kiss her.

Hooded blue eyes regarded her, their expression flicked her senses raw. A pulse beat angrily above his cheek-bone as the austerely-sculpted mouth bent in response.

No welching—she had invited this. But, dear merciful God—not *like* this. She didn't know what had triggered it off—what had she done, *said* to unleash this beast? His mouth insulted hers. It was hard and demanding and it laughed at her—with her lips pressed up close she could feel it laughing—because she couldn't deny the explosive feeling ripping her apart.

He had only ever kissed her once before, the time the Rocas were dining and he'd come to her room to fetch her because their arrival was imminent, and that had been an improper peck. Their first proper kiss should have been a paradisical experience, not this degrading grappling of lips that both sickened and excited. She resisted; he pulled her closer until the unyielding hardness of his body pained her flesh. His hands chafed, *and caressed.* He kissed her until her mouth hurt with the joy of it, and her knees were water. Never in her life had she been brought to such shame; never before had her dignity been dragged to this low of degradation. *He was using her.* She was a body and a pair of lips to satisfy his lust. He wasn't holding her in respect.

A final wrench and she was free to examine his face. Strangely, she could see no apology in his eyes. It was a two-way scrutiny. After that shameful display which had debased everything good that had gone between them, surely he didn't expect to see anything to his advantage in her face? Her breath expelled slowly. Yes . . . he did! She got the distinct impression that he expected her to look repentant.

Her twisting chin was expressive of her bewilderment. He either couldn't, or wouldn't, see.

'With you or without you, I am going to inform the Rocas that their daughter is here.'

'With me.' He wasn't getting away so easily. She had some probing to do.

'You're not afraid to come with me? After . . .?' His eyebrows lifted in mockery; his manner was insulting as to be inflammatory, also slightly surprised.

Why was she cringing? It should have been him. There was a distinct boot-on-the-other-foot flavour about the situation that disturbed even as it intrigued.

After all, it would not wait until she'd been upstairs for her clothes and they were on their way to the Rocas'. The question wouldn't be delayed a moment longer.

'Precisely what did Paco Garcia tell you?'

An earlier question of Carlos's that had fallen on stony ground, was just beginning to take root. 'What has Isabel got to do with this?' he had asked. 'Everything,' Dorcas had replied. What if she was wrong? Something had sent him into a white-hot temper. What could it be, if not Isabel and Paco's sudden acknowledgement of their love for each other? If it had nothing to do with Isabel, could it . . . perhaps . . . have something to do with her?

Carlos had behaved very badly just now. He hadn't kissed her in tenderness, but like a man bitterly wronged, demented by jealousy, seeking lustful revenge. Carlos jealous? Carlos acting like a green boy drooling over his first love? Not jealous of Paco because of Isabel, but jealous of . . .

Oh dear. If Paco had told Carlos something about her, it could only be one thing. Paco had seen her kissing Tom Bennett. Was this enough to make Carlos jealous? Had that silly, meaningless kiss provoked all this? No. It wasn't possible.

'Paco told you he'd seen Tom Bennett and me kissing,' she said, rashly answering her own question.

Reading his expression, she knew she'd blundered. 'No,' he said coldly, 'he didn't tell me that.'

'Oh. I can explain,' she said trying her hopeful best to retrieve the situation. But could she explain? If she remembered rightly, there had been something of an experimental nature about that kiss. She had led Tom on to kiss her in the hope that it would blot out thoughts of Carlos. She coloured. After all, she could not explain that.

'In the circumstances, isn't an explanation both tedious and unnecessary. After all, you'd have a harder job explaining to Tom about us,' he said drily.

'What do you mean?'

'Well, he is your fiancé, isn't he?'

'Who told you that?'

'Paco did.'

'It's not true. Do you think he assumed we

220

were engaged because he saw us kissing?'

'Tom Bennett told Paco you were his fiancée.'

'Why would he tell him that?'

For someone brought up to tell the exact truth, Dorcas wasn't used to extricating herself from lies. Even Michael's inventive tongue couldn't have topped this one.

'Wait a minute, I do believe . . .' Oh, what a tangled web! 'I mentioned to Tom that I was worried that Paco might tell that he'd seen us kissing. Tom said he knew just the word to say to Paco to ensure that he didn't. He must have thought that pretending I was Jane would make things right.'

'Jane?'

'Tom's fiancée from England. She was due to arrive the next day.'

'Really!' said Carlos, sceptically.

'Whatever that's supposed to mean, she does exist. I've met her. On our way back from taking your grandmother home, your father and I narrowly missed hitting a small boy. Tom's fiancée was there. I was afraid of what the shock might do to your father, so I came home with him while Tom's fiancée stayed with the boy. You can check if you like.' A fiery tone entered her voice. 'Shall I tell you something, I don't care whether you believe me or not!' She was weary of explanations. Weary and prickly.

He picked her hand off the newel post

where it had been resting. Thoughtfully his thumb stroked over her wrist. 'We'll talk later. We are both too emotionally wound up to reason clearly.'

Dorcas said: 'Very well,' without much hope.

What did Carlos think? That she and Michael and Tom were all in this together? It would be common knowledge that Tom Bennett was making a home for when his fiancée could join him. Her arrival on the scene could fit. Did Carlos think she had discarded Tom because she saw him as a better prospect and that Tom was willing to step down on peaceable terms . . . in the hope that Enrique Ruiz would keep his promise to put some business his way? All the angles fitted too well. Even that joke proposal of Tom's, which they'd mentioned to Carlos's father, but which he hadn't properly understood, could backfire on her.

Even as Dorcas thought, hopefully there is still Jane as proof positive, a small voice in her head was telling her that love doesn't have to explain. It believes, no matter how damning the evidence.

Dorcas heard the ringing of the doorbell, the rat-tat of heels across the hall, muted voices. Automatically, her head turned.

The Spanish maid was ushering someone in. Unbelievably, it was Jane!

Only Jane was saying: 'How is Michael? I

couldn't stay away, not when I heard he was hurt. I had to come.'

'Of course. Please do not upset yourself.' The comfort Carlos offered wanted no explanation. His voice was warm, yet authoritative, the arrogance subdued to a pleasing acceptance of command. 'Shall you wait in the *sala* with my mother.'

His dictatorial bearing had become solid reassurance that did not come amiss, as verified by the leap of gratitude in the girl's eyes.

'Thank you, señor. That is very kind of you.'

Dorcas had jumped to a wrong conclusion.

The girl who was not Jane said: 'I'm Samantha Harris.' Her eyes reached beseechingly round to Dorcas. 'I know you're Michael's sister. Perhaps he's mentioned me? I'm Michael's fiancée.'

CHAPTER TEN

Samantha Harris had glossy, nutbrown hair, a sunburnt nose, and hazel eyes. The latter were directing Dorcas a look that was marginally apologetic, with a definite bias towards hurt.

'Sorry if it came as a shock. I took it you knew. That time in town—you know, when that cute little Spanish boy, Pepe, nearly ran under your car—I thought you seemed to know who I was.'

'I thought I did. The man who owns the English garage was expecting his fiancée from England. I assumed that's who you were.'

'So Michael never mentioned me?'

She looked so hurt that Dorcas was pleased to be able to say: 'Do you know, I believe he did. He told me he'd met someone called Sam while he was in France. I assumed you were a man. I seem to be making a lot of wrong assumptions lately.'

Her eyes strayed to Carlos who was coming out of a most thoughtful look.

He said, predictably, 'That is unimportant. What matters is that Miss Harris is here and that we make her welcome.'

His smile was doing that quite substantially, the evidence of which showed in the lowering of Samantha's defensive shield and an infinitesimally slight lessening of her woebegone expression.

He might not have Michael's surface charm, but he emanated a protective warmth and strength that was, to Dorcas's way of thinking, far superior. Michael's charm was a flashy gold plating; Carlos's unpretentious twenty-two carat goodness and caring was no illusion. Not that Samantha would be comparing. She saw Carlos merely as a ballast to grasp in her uncertainty and misery.

Her: 'Thank you,' was heartfelt. And then, as though propelled by truth: 'I might not be very welcome with Michael. As a matter of fact, I'm not even certain we're still engaged. It was wonderful in France. No doubts. But then he came here and he only sent me two scrappy postcards. All they told me was how much he was taken up by all this. I wasn't his new plaything any more; this was. I thought if I didn't follow him, he might forget me. But as it turned out it wasn't such a good idea. Oh, he pretended to make a fuss of me at first, and he even helped me to find lodgings in town. He explained, very kindly, why he couldn't make it known I was here. I didn't properly understand what he was getting at, apart from the fact that I'd upset his plans. I feel a bit let-down that he didn't tell you about me. But, I suppose that's just the mystery of Michael.'

'I couldn't have put it better myself,' Dorcas admitted. She thought that no one would ever know exactly what Michael had in mind.

It seemed obvious that he didn't want Samantha's presence known because he was making a play for Isabel. But whether he was doing this because he thought he had a chance with Isabel, or—beautiful and profound thought!—to give her (Dorcas) a chance with Carlos, would never be known to anyone but Michael himself.

She realized where her thoughts had taken her. For the first time she had credited her brother with a magnanimous gesture.

'I know he loves you,' she told Samantha.

Her reward was the look of bliss that came to Samantha's eye, even though it was quickly lost in disbelief. 'How can you know that? He's never told you.'

'Not in so many words. But it's been apparent in his manner. I don't think Michael will ever be a completely reformed character— that's too much to expect—but he's different. He's a nicer, more caring, warmer person. I noticed this the moment he came here; I even asked him if he'd met someone while on holiday to account for it. He has changed, Samantha, and it's entirely due to your influence.'

'Oh, you're just saying that to be kind.'

'It wouldn't be kind to give you false hope.'

'It's not your sincerity I'm doubting. It's just that I can't believe it's true.'

'Don't take my word for it. Wait. And let Michael tell you himself.'

'Oh yes!' The colour drained from Samantha's face as her eyes dredged up the very real fear. She seemed to sway a little. 'I want to wait and hear what Michael has to say. He can tell me to go away if he wants. The important thing is . . . that . . . he . . . can . . .' Her teeth caught on her lower lip, her eyes were swimming. 'What I'm trying to ask is . . . will . . . he . . .' She couldn't say it.

Dorcas put her arms round the girl she hoped one day would be her beloved sister-in-law, and hugged her extravagantly. Samantha had made a big impression on her, and it was this that decided her to chance such a very rash and glowing reply. 'Michael will get well. I promise that he'll be up and about in no time. You'll see. And he'll endorse every word I've said. Just remember to ask me to be bridesmaid.'

A short while later the doctor delivered his verdict on Michael. It came over sweetly and clearly that the professional opinion coincided with hers.

A hand touched her arm. Her glance fastened momentarily on the long, capable fingers before she dragged her eyes up to meet his.

Carlos said: 'I'm glad it isn't as serious with Michael as we first thought. About the other . . .'

Even though that recent, angry, emotional scene was still vividly at the forefront of memory, the embarrassment was not as keen as Dorcas would have expected. She could meet the apology in his eyes. It was the hurt in them she found herself flinching away from. They'd both hurt each other so badly. Dorcas found her breath catching on the hope that the damage done was not irreparable.

'Obviously we can't talk about it in depth here. And there is so much to talk about.'

'Can't we just forget it?' said Dorcas, shrinking from the thought of a heavy discussion. She had no shield to raise against him. She felt vulnerable. Having witnessed its calming effect while everybody was so worried about Michael, she could no longer find it in her to resent his dictatorial manner. And that aura of masculine superiority that she so often chafed against—well—it was indigenous to him. Without it he would have been like a glove without fingers. He wouldn't have been Carlos.

And he wouldn't have been Carlos now without that renegade gleam of humour in his eye. At the same time, not to deflect from the gravity of the situation, his brow was down.

'It can never totally be forgotten, Dorcas.'

'No,' she admitted dismally.

'I behaved very badly. Nothing I can say will ever fully erase the shame of my actions.'

'I can see your side of it, Carlos. At least I'm trying to. You seemed to be of the impression that the three of us, that is Tom, Michael and myself, had cooked something up against you. We hadn't, honestly. As for my being Tom's fiancée, I'd never set eyes on him before that day my hired car broke down and I went to his garage for help. That's the truth. I wasn't trying to pass Samantha off as Tom's fiancée to make my own story credible. I honestly mistook her identity.'

'I know you did. You knew Bennett was expecting his fiancée; you saw Samantha about the town. It was a natural enough mistake. It was a bigger mistake on my part to let myself be driven by blind jealousy. When Paco innocently let slip that he'd seen you before, at Bennett's garage, and that you were Bennett's fiancée no less, I saw red. We won't go into whatever hanky-panky was going on between you and Bennett that led him to claim you as his fiancée. If I'd stopped to think I would have seen how absurd my accusation was. Dearest Dorcas, anyone with an eye less on the main chance I have yet to meet. That has been a major source of irritation.' He broke off to warn her, 'I'm afraid we are about to be interrupted. Here comes Mother.'

Dorcas turned to see Rose Ruiz bearing down on them. The toil and torment of the night showed in her less than immaculate hair, the lines of strain round her mouth, the tiredness dulling her eyes. Even so she was conscientiously pulling out all the stops to be the perfect hostess.

'Dorcas, I think we should provide a meal for our departing guests to see them on their way. Indeed, I think we could all do to appease the hunger pangs after the anxiety. Do you feel up to giving a hand?'

'Of course, señora.'

Rose Ruiz smiled before moving away, obviously expecting Dorcas to follow her. Dorcas hesitated. She had little doubt that she looked as raw and puzzled as she felt.

'What did you mean, Carlos? What has been a major source of irritation?'

'The role you have given me. I am not a Lord Bountiful. I have never regarded you as an object of charity. Neither have I wanted to do things for you out of a misguided sense of obligation. This is ridiculous! We can't talk about it now. It's too public. We'll talk later.'

Rose Ruiz turned round, suddenly aware that Dorcas wasn't immediately behind her. She saw Dorcas lift herself on tiptoe to kiss Carlos on the cheek. Protectively her eyes searched the room for her husband. Enrique had not missed that revealing, tender moment. He was looking fixedly at Dorcas and Carlos; his expression reflected interest, not displeasure. Rose Ruiz permitted herself a small contented sigh.

Dorcas walked away, following the course of Rose Ruiz's steps, feeling curiously light-headed. Too much anxiety, too little food, might have contributed, but the main cause of her affliction was the look on Carlos's face as she spontaneously reached up to kiss his cheek. She didn't know why she'd done it. It had been an impulse. Definitely one of her better ones.

The impromptu meal went down well. Even those who said they weren't hungry found lively appetites.

Paco said he would take Isabel home. They walked out into a new day that was just misting into light, relief that Michael was going to get well nudging back their smiles, fingers tightly linked.

Rose Ruiz accepted Samantha's presence in their midst without fuss, and with minimal explanation. She gave orders for a room to be prepared for the unexpected guest. Samantha made a token protest. 'Are you sure it's not too much of an imposition?' At the same time she looked as if it would take a bulldozer to evict her before she'd spoken to Michael.

Enrique Ruiz sought out his wife. 'My Rose is wilting. There is nothing more to be done. Let us go to bed.'

'Are you quite sure you are all right, Enrique? The strain hasn't been too much for you?'

'I've never felt fitter. If I can come through this night of shocks and feel like this, you must see how silly it is of you to worry about me.'

'Indulge me, Enrique, you are so dear to me I can't help worrying.'

'No regrets?'

'None. Enrique?'

'Yes, *querida*?'

'I might worry about you less if you handed more of the running of the business over to Carlos. You do too much. And surely he's proved his capability?'

'Indubitably he has. It's taken me a long time to come round to admitting it, but in the running of the business, and in other things, Carlos knows best.'

Rose Ruiz knew it was the 'other things' that Enrique was mainly thinking about.

She said: 'You saw Dorcas kiss Carlos on the cheek. You didn't mind?'

He smiled. 'I saw Isabel and Paco holding hands.'

Rose Ruiz mentally hugged herself. 'I saw that too.'

'You know what it means, don't you?' His eyes were suspiciously shiny. 'It means the debt is now paid in full. *Gracias a Dios*, we are not going to be asked to pay a second time. And now, *amor de mi vida*, come to bed.'

The love of his life put her hand in his, and they turned towards the stairs.

* * *

Samantha was with Michael when the effects of the tranquillizer the doctor had administered wore off. True, he still looked

232

gravely ill, but the smile he gave her was a heartwarmingly contented one.

'Hello, Sam. Glad you're here.' Sincerity outstripped eloquence. Not even Samantha, with all her suspicions, could have doubted him.

Her breath sucked in furiously. 'I'm glad to be here. Go back to sleep love, if you want to. I'll still be here when you wake up.'

'That's nice.' So saying, he closed his eyes and fell into a natural, healing sleep.

Samantha utilized the time by making plans. 'I'm taking him home to meet my parents as soon as he's fit enough to travel. He can get to know them while he's recuperating. At the same time he can decide what he's going to do with his life.'

Obviously, with Samantha at the helm, Michael's aimless drifting days were over. Dorcas felt happy about this; at peace. She couldn't remember the last time she'd felt this easy in her mind about her brother.

Samantha was so precisely right for him. She'd always thought he would settle down with a fragile beauty to complement his own special looks, and they would spend their lives getting out of one pretty pickle after another. Samantha was neither fragile, nor beautiful. Not even pretty. But there was a sturdy, glossy wholesomeness about her that was most attractive. She had depth of character. Her smile didn't merely charm her lips, but

233

warmed her whole face. She was older than Michael, and made no secret of the fact that she had been considering dusting the shelf when he came along. Yet there was no question of her having grabbed a 'last chance'. She idolized him, faults and all.

Carlos was not so impressed. When Dorcas said: 'Isn't she lovely?' he wrinkled his nose and replied: 'Much too bossy for my taste.'

Dorcas wondered how he of all people dare say that. Not one word to this effect crossed her lips, but the look she darted him was based on this thought.

He interpreted it well. Using that smug, intolerably overbearing tone that made her teeth feel as though they were being brushed with sandpaper, he said: 'That trait is acceptable, even desirable in a man.'

This conversation was taking place in the library, the one room where they had a fair chance of being undisturbed. When Carlos increased the odds in favour of this by going over and closing the door, Dorcas knew it was time for that promised talk.

She both welcomed it and dreaded it.

'Do you find me impossibly arrogant?' he asked.

'No.'

Somehow she knew that wasn't the most vital issue. She might fight his attitude and insist she would dance to no man's tune, but it was the other thing she didn't properly

234

understand that wouldn't let them harmonize.

He said, getting to the crux of the matter, 'We haven't got the balance right. We tip too easily into misunderstanding.'

She nodded. 'I feel so confused.'

'Please don't look so worried.'

He reached out a hand in comfort, his fingers cherished the contours of her face. It was such a protective captivity that her bones melted in delight. His cheek rested briefly against hers, then she felt her chin being tilted. His face blurred before her eyes. She would never know how she managed to find the will to tear her mouth from the proximity of his, but the kiss that would have brooked no holding back on her part was averted.

'No, Carlos. Not this way, with nothing resolved. Don't you see, I've got to understand?'

'I'm sorry. I don't normally believe in taking short cuts, but this time it seemed a better choice than going the long way round. We have a habit of coming up against hazards.'

She had noticed.

He leaned his chin on his hands, looking cool, English, and unruffled. Perversely, she preferred the hotheaded Spaniard. She wished she hadn't deflected him.

'I don't know where to start,' he said.

'The beginning?' she suggested.

'The beginning was all right. There were problems, yes. But none that I couldn't get a

235

grip of. The moment I saw you, when you gatecrashed my parents' anniversary tea, I knew I wanted to know you better. You were terribly upset because you'd mistaken a private villa for a public tea garden. Short of nailing you to the chair, I couldn't stop you from going. As the roads were blocked because of the landslide, your only means of escape was by train, and it just so happened that my sister was planning to go home on the next train that was due out. So I knew there was more than a chance of seeing you again. You kept well hidden on the platform. I didn't spot you until the last possible moment when you slipped on to the train. My sister, Feli, had seen you earlier when you wandered into our garden by mistake. She'd already pulled my leg about my being taken with you, so all it needed was a word in her ear to ensure her full cooperation. But why are you looking so surprised? You surely didn't think that it was coincidence that made Feli sit opposite you on an almost empty train?'

'Well . . . I realize how stupid I must seem . . . but yes! Wait a minute, though, Feli didn't recognize me straight away.'

'I've no idea how she played it. I told her to go easy so as not to scare you off.'

'Feli asked me to stay with her for part of my holiday. Are you saying she didn't ask me on impulse, but that she was following your instructions?'

236

'I wasn't twisting her arm, you know. Feli would have enjoyed *using* you. You would have earned your keep acting as unpaid nursemaid to my small niece. No, I'm not being fair. Feli loves company. But, when you turned her down, she didn't press the issue. And, well, you know what happened then.'

'Yes. Part of the mountainside crumbled to block the railway track and the train ran into an avalanche of rock and earth and sludge.'

'When word got back I nearly went out of my mind. I felt as if I'd wished this terrible thing on you. Before that it had been a rather pleasant game. You were on holiday, I was at a loose end; it had all the makings of an amusing interlude. Then suddenly it turned into this tragic reality. When I first came to sit with you in hospital it was to make amends. It could no longer be an amusing interlude, and I had no wish for a deeper involvement. I hadn't reckoned with . . . well . . . you can't be with someone all these hours, hurt for them, feel for them, without feeling something yourself. I wasn't looking too far into the future just then. We had gone through a very emotional period together; for the time being I was just satisfied to be taking you home.'

Realization came in a rush. 'And I couldn't have made it plainer that I didn't want to come home with you.'

'I remember your very words. You said, "I am not returning with you voluntarily to your home. Circumstance has put me in the invidious position of having no alternative." '

'Did I say that? I didn't mean . . .'

'I could have been taking you to a prison for all the joy on your face. I wanted to wipe that trapped look from your eyes, but how could I when I was responsible for keeping you against your will? Then again, what alternative did I have? Nobody was trying to repay you for what you did for Feli and Rosita, because there's no price to be put on that. You were hurt and alone, but even if you'd had an army of relatives I'd still have fought for the privilege. Believe me, I *wanted* to take care of you.'

'Oh . . . Carlos . . . don't. I can't . . . bear . . .'

'Hush, I didn't mean to distress you. Proud and stubborn you might be, but the tenderness of your heart has never been in dispute. Dorcas, please don't let anyone, least of all me, tie any more knots in your emotions. At first I thought it was because you were alone in a strange country. I moved heaven and earth to get your brother here, because I thought his presence would give you the necessary anchor, the illusion of home. I still think that theory was right as far as it went, it didn't go far enough that's all. You need to sort out your feelings with your feet firmly planted on the ground. Home ground, if you like. Would you like to go home?'

'Home?' Dorcas echoed stupidly. For a long time now, longer than she realized, home wasn't England. Home was here with Carlos.

'I haven't quite made up my mind whether I am being self-sacrificing about this, or selfish. I do know it's a situation that calls for patience. I refuse to burden a decision of this magnitude on a small emotional yes, and I'm not going to risk a no. So you can relax. You're not going to be rushed or made to do anything against your will.'

He was wrong. He was proposing to send her home. That was against her will.

'I'm sorry, Carlos. I didn't mean to appear rude and ungrateful.'

She had never meant to throw his kindness back in his face, but that's how it must have looked to him. No wonder he wanted to be rid of her. Oh! he'd wrapped it up in kind words, but the message was clear. Her seeming ingratitude had cost her dearly. It had lost her Carlos. The sun must have been in her eyes for her not to see that loving is caring and giving. She knew that had it been the other way round, if she had been the fortunate one, she would have wanted to give everything she had to Carlos. She had made it plain she wanted nothing from him. And so, because of her stupidity, he would never give her the one thing she wanted most of all. That priceless gift that had to be offered by him to have any meaning . . . the gift of love.

'It's all settled then. I'll make the arrangements.'

239

The words begging him not to send her away remained locked in that block of ice she called her throat.

She felt the brush of his lips against her cheek. When she looked up, he had gone.

*   *   *

'Dorcas, what are you doing hiding in here on such a lovely day? I was quite convinced you'd gone for a walk, otherwise I would have fetched you to pay your respects to Isabel's mama. She's gone now, of course.'

After answering Rose Ruiz's smile—and a very self-satisfied smile it was at that—Dorcas said: 'I'd no idea she was here. Was Isabel with her?'

'No, doña Maria came alone. We had quite a long and illuminating chat. I knew she hadn't come solely to enquire after your brother. All the same, I was more than a little surprised at what she had to tell me.' Her mouth curved. She looked girlishly smug in her appreciation of what had transpired.

Impulsively she said: 'It's too delicious not to share, and it will be common knowledge soon enough anyway. Even so, I wouldn't discuss something so private if I didn't consider you one of the family. And in this I speak for both Enrique and myself. Well—!'

And before Dorcas could blink her gratification away, she plunged into her story.

240

'As you know, Paco took Isabel home. According to doña Maria, instead of leaving her at the door, he went in for the confrontation. He didn't ask for Isabel's hand in marriage, doña Maria said he demanded it. Don Alfonso looked angry enough to strike him. Isabel began to cry. Doña Maria said she didn't know what to do. Bearing in mind that she is very Spanish, and has spent her entire life first echoing the thoughts and wishes of her father and then her husband, it must have taken a great deal of courage for her to speak up for the young lovers. I must admit she did this in an intriguing and subtle way. You won't understand all this, Dorcas. Until you know the full story it can't possibly make sense. All I ask is that you hear me out and I promise to fill in the blanks later. Anyway, doña Maria drew in a deep breath and said, "Alfonso, are we in a position to condemn them? It has come full circle, only this time the shame is ours." And then she said, "Can you look into your heart and honestly say that you would change what happened all those years ago?" And he replied with tears in his eyes, "No, my dear. You quickly allayed any doubts I might have had by letting me know exactly where I stood with you. I might not have been first choice but it wasn't long before I occupied first place in your heart".' Rose Ruiz sighed. 'Don't you find that just too touching, Dorcas?'

Dorcas, who was having difficulty in

swallowing, merely nodded.

'What could don Alfonso add to that moving little speech except his blessing to the young couple. Then he got to worrying that it might stop the merger between our two family concerns. So doña Maria came to ask me to help square things with Enrique and Carlos. As I told doña Maria, Enrique could hardly put up a protest in the circumstances. Have patience, Dorcas, you'll soon appreciate the irony of it, but I'm afraid all this talk has made me thirsty.'

And so curiosity had to be held in check while tea was brought.

Dorcas wondered if Rose Ruiz's need to occupy her hands with the tea things wasn't greater than her desire for liquid refreshment. The telling wasn't easy and circumnavigated the main issue until it didn't seem part of the same story.

'It was silly of us to be wary of you, wasn't it, Dorcas? We should have settled back and let time take its own course.'

Was it apparent even to his mother that Carlos had lost interest in her? And wasn't it just a little cruel of Rose Ruiz to highlight this fact? Yet, search as she might Dorcas saw no intent to hurt in the older woman's eyes, and she heard only the voice of candour.

'Now that the worry aspect has been removed, I don't mind admitting that your arrival stirred the memories, and the guilt.

Enrique and I never should have married. Don't misunderstand me. It's been a wonderful marriage, a perfect partnership. It needed to be to survive. Like Carlos, Enrique was pledged to marry the daughter of a family friend and business colleague. He shocked everyone by not marrying her, and marrying me instead. The girl didn't love Enrique, and I suspect she was even glad to be released from a "suitable" marriage. Those immediately concerned retained a sense of proportion. It was the outsiders who created the fuss. So, perhaps now you see why we were wary of you. It looked as though it was going to happen all over again. Having lived through it once, we knew the difficulties you would face.'

All this coincided with the things don Enrique had told her that time in his study. Dorcas knew that Rose Ruiz was taking the confidence a step further. Something about to be revealed to her would tie everything up.

'Perhaps I'm being imaginative, but it's almost as if you were looking to a marriage between Carlos and Isabel to put things right. This I don't understand.'

'It's not imaginative of you at all, Dorcas. It's very perceptive. And you will understand when you know the name of the girl Enrique should have married.'

In the pause that followed, Dorcas gathered her wits and was stirred to make a second observation. 'You speak as though it's

243

someone I know.'

'It is. Haven't you guessed? It's Isabel's mama. That's what makes it so ironic. Enrique broke his engagement to Maria to marry me, severely straining, almost severing it seemed at one point, a family friendship that had been handed down from generation to generation. And now the boot is on the other foot. Seemingly, Isabel is jilting Carlos to marry Paco. As Carlos never intended to marry Isabel in the first place, this time we have come out of it remarkably well.'

'I see it all now, but I would never have guessed. I didn't suspect anything like this. You never let it make any difference. You were always so kind to me. It makes me feel unworthy. No, please—' When Rose Ruiz would have stopped her. 'You must let me finish. I didn't realize, until it was pointed out to me recently, that I might have appeared ungrateful. I am grateful to you for having me and showing me so much kindness.'

'My dear, I find your confession both sweet and touching, and totally unnecessary. I understand you far better than you think. You can't help being as you are any more than Michael can help being as he is. I have no doubt your grandmother was a wise woman in many ways, but she had her blind spots. She didn't do either of you any good by always putting Michael first. No, nobody told me this.'—Answering Dorcas's look of surprise.

'Who is there to tell? It's just obvious, that's all. I can't see much hope for Michael. Like every other besotted female he's come across, and that doesn't exclude me, Samantha will want to spoil him. He could charm a smile out of stone, that one. He'll always be liked, in spite of his shortcomings. And I'm not all that worried about you. You haven't had a fair crack at life. The man you marry is going to have a lot of fun making it up to you.'

She paused to sip her tea. Rattling her cup back in her saucer with none of her usual care, she seemed to bend to an overwhelming compulsion. 'I hope it's Carlos. I shouldn't be saying this. I know I'm speaking out of turn, but I can't keep it back. When I said just now that I considered you family, it wasn't just because I find you a kindred spirit. I hope you will be family. I do so dearly hope that Carlos has the good sense to marry you. I know I couldn't wish for a sweeter daughter-in-law.' She leaned forward to kiss Dorcas's—by this time—damp cheek.

Dorcas brushed the tears away with the back of her hand, as a child might have done. She was a child again, remembering a moment long ago when her own mother had pulled her close in just such a spontaneous gesture. Her mother had never made any difference between her and Michael. The past was too painful. She pushed it back where it belonged.

Concentrating hard she said: 'I don't think

that is very likely.'

'Oh dear! Have you had a lovers' tiff?'

For answer Dorcas bit hard on her lip. 'Lovers' tiff' sounded like a small dissent that could easily be resolved. Their difference went much deeper than that. Try as she might, she couldn't see a happy making-up.

A hand came comfortingly down on hers. 'I shouldn't worry too much. Things have a knack of coming right.'

Some things were too wrong ever to come right. It seemed ironical that now it was right with Carlos's parents, it was wrong between them.

*　　　*　　　*

When several days elapsed and Carlos still hadn't said anything about getting her plane reservation, Dorcas decided he wasn't going to send her home while Michael was so ill. It was the sort of considerate gesture she had come to expect of Carlos. What struck her as being out of character was the new and not totally acceptable soberness about him these days. Yet she could have sworn that somewhere at the back of that unduly grave expression was a locked-in smile. Yes. Very strange.

Michael had youth on his side, and a tip-top constitution to start with. He soon got better. He complained of getting headaches, but was assured these would clear in the time it took

246

his hair to grow to its original length. They'd cut away the hair round the gash in his head in order to stitch it. This had given him a rather lop-sided appearance which only severe, all round cutting had resolved. He looked even sweeter and more angelic than ever with very short hair.

Each day found Carlos more deeply involved with a heavier work load. It wasn't just the merger; he was shouldering a larger slice of responsibility than he had previously borne. It was a result of the merger that an opening occurred for a liaison man. Carlos offered the position to Michael. A move that did not altogether surprise Dorcas, because Alfonso Roca had spotted Michael out as a bright prospect some time earlier. Michael's appointment would be with don Alfonso's approval now that Isabel was officially engaged to Paco, and Michael was no longer a threat. Urged by Samantha, he accepted. And now Samantha and Michael were making wedding plans, and searching the district for a modestly priced villa. There was nothing to keep Dorcas now, and she lived in daily dread of being handed her air ticket home.

She called at the garage to tell Tom Bennett that she expected to be going home quite soon. She was sorry to learn that things hadn't worked out for him and Jane. He revealed the contents of the letter his eyes had strayed to on her previous visit. Instead of informing him of the date of her arrival as Tom had led Dorcas to believe, Jane had written to say it would be like coming out to marry a stranger. She said the separation had been needlessly long, that if they'd really wanted each other they would have found a way. She wrote that the only thing left to say was—and this was the message of Jane's letter—goodbye.

'And she's right,' Tom said sagely. 'We couldn't have wanted it enough, or we would have made it happen.'

It made Dorcas think again about Tom's lightly worded proposal of marriage to her. Had it entirely been the joke she had taken it for? Was it, just possibly, the tentative thoughts of a recently jilted man, motivated by loneliness? She would never know. Neither did she want to. She liked Tom, she would always remember him as a friend, but the vital spark was missing. When she left, promising to convey his thanks to Enrique Ruiz who had kept his word about putting some business Tom's way, she was careful not to kiss him goodbye.

She arrived back at the villa to be told by Rose Ruiz: 'You've just missed Isabel and her mama.'

'I wish I'd known. I would have hurried back. Are they well? Is doña Maria bearing up?'

'Only just. Isabel is a dear girl. At the moment she's bubbling over with joy. She's like champagne. Can you imagine a regular diet of champagne? Come talk to me, Dorcas. On any subject but weddings. Unless—?'

There was blatant appeal in Rose Ruiz's eyes. Dorcas had nothing to tell her. At least, not the thing that Rose Ruiz seemed to want to know.

'Did you know that Carlos was arranging to get my plane ticket home?'

Rose Ruiz thought about it for a moment. Comprehension touched her features like a golden glow. 'Yes dear,' she said, to Dorcas's intense surprise.

It was contradictory, surely? If the señora knew that Carlos was sending her home, how could she cling to the belief that their differences were as good as settled? It didn't make sense. It was even odder than the strange, even smug expression Carlos wore these days.

'Carlos is up to something,' she said speculatively. 'I don't know what, but he's planning something.'

'I shouldn't worry about it. Whatever it is, it's sure to include you.'

There it was again, that firm belief that they had a future together, when all the facts pointed against it.

'Carlos is said to favour me in looks, but he is like his father in many ways. They both adore springing surprises. Without breaking faith, I can tell you that at the moment they are acting like a pair of grown-up children. At such times it's best to humour them. Now, my husband was looking for you earlier. If you go at once, I think you will find he is still in his study.'

'Do you know what he wants me for?'

'That comes under the heading of Awkward Questions. I'm pretending like mad that I don't know anything is going on. I honestly don't *know*.'

Her mouth was a curve of blissful satisfaction.

'But you've guessed.'

'It comes with practise. Over the years I've become adept at picking up the clues. For example, you wouldn't believe what you have told me just now. It's what I suspected; you confirmed it. No, don't ask me. I've said too much as it is.' Knocking tentatively on the study door, pushing it open, Dorcas said: 'Did you want to see me, señor?'

'Ah, yes, Dorcas! Come in and shut the door behind you. I want to show you something.' When he added: 'It's a surprise,' she had to suppress a smile. 'I want the feminine viewpoint on a present I have bought for my wife's birthday.'

It was a necklace of sapphires and turquoises.

'You do not think it is perhaps too ornate for my English Rose?' the señor asked anxiously.

250

'No, no señor. It's in impeccable taste. The señora will love it.' Her approval shone through her enchanted eyes. 'When is the señora's birthday?'

'On the sixteenth of this month. In Spain, we do not celebrate birthdays as you do. We celebrate our saint's day. My Rose insists on her English birthright to celebrate her birthday. It is good, yes? We have two countries, two sets of customs.'

'Yes, señor, it is good.'

'My Rose's birthday is always special.' He smiled on a private thought. 'This year it will be even more special than usual. As you will see, Dorcas.'

Rose Ruiz was right. Don Enrique was acting like a grown-up child.

Dorcas had already bought parting presents for everyone. For Rose Ruiz the had chosen an antelope carved in wood, poised as for flight. Carlos had once likened her to a gazelle. She hoped that sometimes he would look at it and think of her. It would have been too obvious to give the wooden animal to Carlos. She still had a little money left, so she would buy the señora an extra gift for her birthday. Something personal and frivolous. Perfume perhaps.

Later that same day, Carlos handed her the dreaded plane ticket which would take her home.

I look the same, she thought whimsically, but I'm not me. This man has taken me apart, and put me together again. Outside, I look nice and tidy and composed. Inside, I don't know where anything is. My independent spirit is there somewhere, but I can't find it.

'What date is my flight?'

He seemed to be regarding her closely. 'The fourteenth.'

She had expected more grace. A week, even longer. 'That's in two days' time,' she gasped, her composure sabotaged by the finality of it all. 'It's just that—' Searching for a plausible explanation to account for her distress—'I'll miss your mother's birthday.'

'By what misguided thought did you arrive at that?'

'Can we start again, please. You've just lost me.'

'That, my love, is precisely what I am safeguarding against not doing.'

'This is crazy! Your mother's birthday is on the sixteenth? Right?'

'Right.'

'Well . . . if I'm going home on the fourteenth . . . ? I don't understand.'

'In Spain, birthdays are considered of less importance than one's saint's day. Were you aware of this?'

'I wasn't until your father told me.'

'Mother claims her birthright to celebrate her birthday. This year my father thought it would add a special touch if it was celebrated in the country of her birth.'

'You mean . . . England?'

'I might as well take this back to keep with the rest,' he said, plucking the plane reservation he had just given her out of her hand.

'The rest?'

'I've got tickets for all of us. Grandmother in particular is looking forward to the trip.'

'You mean you are all coming to England to celebrate your mother's birthday?'

He gave her the kind of tolerant smile he might have awarded a much-loved child. 'Yes, of course!'

'So that's what your father meant when he said your mother's birthday was to be even more special this year. It also accounts for that smug look of yours these past few days.'

'Oh? Have I been looking smug then?'

'You know you have.'

His eyes, resting on her so tenderly, were tempting her to hope. Yet when had hope ever fulfilled its promise? Hope beckoned—to disappoint. Tempted—to disdain. Yet here it was, resilient as ever, rising again. This time don't let it bank her into a brick wall. This time, let it be different.

'I thought you were sending me away. I thought you didn't want me any more,' she said in a small voice.

'Sending you away?' he said incredulously. 'Not want you!' He groaned. 'If only you knew!'

'I know you've played a mean trick on me. You deliberately led me to believe what I did.'

'You think I should have told you about the extra birthday surprise my father was planning for Mother? But Dorcas, you must see the secret wasn't mine to divulge. My father went to a lot of trouble to keep it from Mother. You can't deny the two of you are as thick as thieves. Could I risk Mother wheedling it out of you?'

'You are doing it again, Carlos. You know that's not what I meant. Anyway, I think you would have a hard task keeping anything from your mother. The only person who has been in the dark about what's been going on is me.'

'No, you are wrong there, Dorcas. I haven't been too enlightened myself.'

She braced herself. She wanted to enlighten him . . . but how could she enlighten the cautious Englishman without stepping on the arrogant Spaniard's toes? By agreeing, she decided.

'It's like you said about the balance not being right. We have tipped too easily into misunderstanding.'

But not any more. Her expression was both exultant and tender. Of course! Carlos was no ordinary man. In trying to understand him, she hadn't taken into account that by virtue of his English mother and his Spanish father, he was two men. He was Charles, the fun-loving, cautious Englishman. And Carlos,

254

the romantic, arrogant Spaniard. What a devastating combination! And she was hard-pressed to know which she loved best, and it was a bonus to be able to love them both in the same extraordinary, gentle, dominant, compassionate, arrogant man.

'Would you say the balance of understanding was about right now?' Carlos suggested.

He had been studying her face closely, and now it was his expression that seemed to drive the breath from her body.

'Yes.'

'That's what I think.' That arrogant smile played so sweetly about his mouth. 'If I did mislead you—and yes, I intended to a little!—I was also giving you time to sort yourself out. I thought that if I could find the patience to wait until we were in England, I would stand a better chance of getting the response I wanted. I won't take no for an answer.'

'You won't have to, Carlos,' she said shakily.

'My beloved.' The tenderly spoken endearment melted her eyes to tears. 'Yes, you are that, Dorcas. I never meant to keep you in suspense about my feelings.' His hands worked their way up to her elbows and then he drew her the rest of the way into his arms. 'I love you.' He seemed to sigh the words, as if finding a long-awaited release in that so joyously received declaration.

Dorcas took it, this precious gift . . . his love

. . . into her humble and grateful heart.

'I love you too, Carlos.'

'We must never misunderstand each other again. I won't allow it.'

She couldn't resist asking mischievously: 'And what will you do to prevent it? Beat me?'

'No. I'll range our children on my side and outnumber you.'

'Children . . . our children! Oh . . . Carlos.'

'Not straight away, so you can wipe that blissful, maternal look off your face. To begin with I am going to be very selfish and insist on having you all to myself. Aren't you arguing?'

'No.' There was a certain wisdom in what Rose Ruiz said about letting time take its course.

'That's settled then.'

'Not quite, Carlos.'

His puzzled look was quickly replaced by a smile. 'Ah . . . yes! As I only intend doing this once, I might as well do it in style.' And now his eyes were solemn to suit the occasion. On bended knee he said: 'Will you do me the honour of becoming my wife?'

'Thank you,' said Dorcas, swallowing hard. 'That was a beautiful thing to do. I'm sure no one proposes like that these days.' Then, realizing, 'Dearest Carlos, of course my answer is yes.'

We hope you have enjoyed this Large Print book. Other Chivers Press or Thorndike Press Large Print books are available at your library or directly from the publishers.

For more information about current and forthcoming titles, please call or write, without obligation, to:

Chivers Large Print
published by BBC Audiobooks Ltd
St James House, The Square
Lower Bristol Road
Bath BA2 3BH
UK
email: bbcaudiobooks@bbc.co.uk
www.bbcaudiobooks.co.uk

OR

Thorndike Press
295 Kennedy Memorial Drive
Waterville
Maine 04901
USA
www.gale.com/thorndike
www.gale.com/wheeler

All our Large Print titles are designed for easy reading, and all our books are made to last.